FRONTIER FREEDOM

ROCKY MOUNTAIN SAINT BOOK 2

B.N. RUNDELL

WOLFPACK
PUBLISHING
— EST 2013 —

Frontier Freedom
(Rocky Mountain Saint Book 2)

B.N. Rundell

Paperback Edition

Wolfpack Publishing

6032 Wheat Penny Avenue

Las Vegas, NV 89122

Cover Design by L.J. Martin

Patience is a virtue. At least on this score, I guess you could say I'm not very virtuous. Patience has never been my strong suit and as a result, I am always amazed and blessed when I am the recipient of that virtue from others. Of course, my beloved has shown an inordinate amount of patience with her most impatient husband for well over half a century. My teachers, my friends, my professors, my congregations, well, just about everybody that has ever stepped into my life, have proven themselves to be patient with me. And for that I am thankful. But especially I am thankful to my Lord and Savior for His patience without limit, His love beyond measure and His promises indescribable. And it is to everyone that has been patient with me that I dedicate this work and may I also beg for more mercy? Thanks everyone!

CHAPTER ONE
BUILDING

TATUM LED THE BIG BAY THROUGH THE TREES AS THEY SNAKED another spruce log to the growing stack near his cabin site. The long days yielded a good start on the logs needed for his first cabin in the Sangre de Cristo mountains. With the bay and his sorrel, he alternated with each of the horses getting a half day's break from the arduous labor of dragging logs to the site. Tatum would spend a day or two cutting and trimming logs, and an equal time snaking them from the deep timber. He was selective with his cutting, making sure the logs he took would not be a giveaway to his homesite. Taking few logs from nearby, the extra work of dragging them any distance would prevent any obvious sign of building in this wild frontier. With several bands of Ute living across the valley to the West, Comanche and Jicarilla Apache to the South and East and the possibility of Arapaho, Cheyenne, and Kiowa coming from beyond the mountains to the East, it was important that he make his presence as inconspicuous as possible.

This would be his first winter in the mountains, and he was careful to heed the advice given him by Kit Carson. The well-known explorer and mountain man was working for William Bent at Bent's Fort on the Sante Fe trail when Tatum met him. When Kit had kind

of taken Tatum under his wing, he freely shared some of his knowledge of the mountains and Indians with the young newcomer to the
Rockies. Now Tatum was on his own and seeking to fulfill a long-held
dream that he shared with his father, to live in the Rocky Mountains
and enjoy a life of freedom. Tatum's mother had died helping to stay a
plague of smallpox that hit the Osage Indians near Cape Girardeau,
Missouri. His father was killed by a crooked card-sharp after Tatum
and Johnathan Saint moved to the small settlement of Springfield
where Johnathan had taken a job as a schoolteacher. Evicted from
their home supplied by the community for the schoolmaster, Tatum
chose to follow his dream and go to the mountains.

On his journey to the West, Tatum had several run-ins with both
Indians and whites and had been treated better by the Osage, Kiowa
and Comanche than the many whites he encountered. This only
further soured him on spending any time with people and solidified
his decision to find a place in the mountains that would provide him
the solitude he longed for and was working toward. As he labored, he
found his thoughts often turning to his memories of his Ma and Pa
and his youth spent in the woods of Missouri. A friend of his youth,
Red Calf, son of Jeremiah Tallchief of the Osage, had spent many
times in the woods with Tatum and shared the knowledge of his
people, and the experiences during his journey West, with the Osage
and Black Buffalo, the Kiowa and Dohäsan and the Comanche and
Buffalo Hump. This had been a full year and it wasn't even close to
being over, winter was coming, and he had lots of work to do in
preparing his winter quarters.

Tatum untied the long-braided hemp rope from the log and coiled
it. He bellied up on the bay and swung his leg over the bare-back
mount and reined around to retrieve the next log. He glanced over his
shoulder at the assortment of logs that lay to the side of the small
clearing and with a quick calculation thought himself to be half way
through the logging part of his job. As he pointed the bay to the rise of
the mountain's shoulder that held the large grove of spruce and fir, he
mentally pictured the needed poles for the roof. He remembered the

large group of lodgepole pine that was farther up the mountain and knew his work wasn't half through. It would take several days to collect the long skinny poles for his roof. He lifted his eyes to the sky and was relieved to see the cloudless blue that he found so common in this country. But as he entered the thicket of Aspen, he was reminded of the rapidly coming winter season as the quakies rattled their golden tinged leaves at his passing.

He had fashioned a sling for his Hawken from his first attempt at tanning a deer hide, and the rifle now hung across his back. The tomahawk, a gift from Black Buffalo of the Osage, was tucked in his belt at his right side, a fringed sheath held his Bowie knife at the small of his back, and his Paterson Colt was secured in the holster at his left hip. Across his chest, the rawhide thongs of his possibles bag and powder horn formed an "X" over the fringed buckskin shirt that dangled over his buckskin britches. The outfit of buckskins had been a gift from Sacred Sun, the wife of Jeremiah Tallchief, and given to him when he left Missouri for the mountains. Now, less than a year later, shirt and britches alike were stretched tight over the growing frame of the young man. Only about three fingers shy of six feet, with shoulders that were showing the muscles of hard work, dark wavy hair that curled just above his collar and arms and hands that showed muscles and calluses of hard work, Tatum was a handsome young man. His size, maturity, and weathered features belied his age of coming on sixteen. He had earned the respect of chiefs in three tribes of Indians and of William Bent and Kit Carson, but his only yearning was to find a solitary life away from people and so-called civilization.

Tatum had been given the name Longbow by the Kiowa, because of his skill with his handcrafted longbow. His father had been a teacher and English history buff that spent his free hours with his son crafting an exact copy of the longbows used by the English and Welsh in medieval warfare. When Tatum demonstrated the superior strength and range of the longbow to the people of the Kiowa, Dohäsan, the chief, gave him the name Longbow. Tatum used the bow often, preferring the silent hunt to preserve the secrecy of his presence.

Arriving at the next downed log, he dropped to the ground and began securing it to drag back to the homesite. After tying off the rope, he turned to the bay and noticed the horse standing rigid, head up and ears forward as he looked through the trees toward the valley floor. Tatum squatted to look below the hanging branches of the nearby pine and saw movement past the edge of the trees about two hundred yards below. His vision was slightly obscured by the thick timber, but as he moved side to side, he saw the movement was a group of the brown woolies, or buffalo. As he watched, he counted eleven cows and calves and three bulls, lazily grazing in the tall grass between the edge of the trees and the willows on the bank of the meandering stream.

Suddenly, the entire herd jumped as one, and started their flight straight across the small stream, trampling the willows as if they were nothing but tall grass. Close on their heels were several mounted Indians, screaming and waving lances and bows with nocked arrows. Tatum was surprised at the action, knowing most hunters would want to get as close as possible and maybe get a shot or two before the herd stampeded, but these were chasing and screaming before they got a shot. But within mere seconds, Tatum heard the blasts from rifles and knew the hunters had set a trap with those that had rifles ready to drop the fleeing animals. He knew the others would pursue the remaining animals and take as many as possible. But what concerned him was these were not the Comanche he knew, but from another tribe, probably Ute. Carson had told him about the different bands of the Ute whose homeland was in the La Garita and San Juan mountains which lay to the west of the San Luis Valley and the Sangre de Cristo. Although Carson had said they were a good people, Tatum could only trust his own experience and so far, he had none with the Ute.

He turned back to his work and led the bay as they snaked another log to the homesite. After each day of snaking logs, Tatum would backtrack and do whatever he could to cover the trail of dragging the logs, knowing he couldn't completely obliterate all signs, but with his efforts and the passage of time, the signs of his passing would dim. By the end of the day, he decided he would need at least another week of logging to secure enough for the walls, and probably another three days to supply the lodgepole for the roof. As he walked around the marked-out location for his cabin, he calculated the work remaining. He had helped his father build a cabin, workshop, and lean-tos for the animals. He remembered the details that would take extra time, splitting logs and making the boards for framing the windows and door, and shutters. He shook his head and looked at the sky again, and muttered a simple prayer, *Lord, I can't do it without Your help. I need time and strength and that can only come from You.*

He rekindled the small cookfire under the long branches of the towering ponderosa. He had the habit of getting the cooking done in the twilight of the day when the smoke, although dispersed by the pine branches, would be less visible and the light of the fire would not bring attention. The small fire warmed the pot of coffee left from breakfast, and the slices of venison hung over the flames, dripping juices into the fire. The rest of the deer haunch hung from a high branch in the ponderosa and was beginning to show more bone than meat. As he looked at it, he knew he would have to do some more hunting, probably first thing in the morning.

He looked around his homesite and smiled as he considered his choice. He had explored this side of the mountains for almost two weeks before he found this place that suited him. A tall cliff face of granite rose high above him for well over a hundred feet and the sheer face defied even the tenuous pinyon from gaining a foothold anywhere. At the very edge of the sheer precipice he could make out a few branches of ponderosa that extended in the air as if trying to shade the granite face. A wide overhang extended out from an undercut of the cliff and gave room for shelter and had probably sheltered other sojourners in the past. Tatum's plan was to build the cabin utilizing the cliff face and overhang as the back wall of the cabin, and extending the other three walls into the clearing. Adjoining the cabin and utilizing the rest of the overhang, he would build a corral and lean-to that would protect his animals and the winter's store of grass that he would harvest from the valley below. There was also a break in the cliff that Tatum had briefly explored, and he thought it would be a good storage for his winter's supply of meat. Although it appeared as an opening to a large cavern, his exploration had been limited by time and light, but he was certain it would suffice for his needs.

It's gonna be a lot of work, but I think it's gonna be a great place when I'm done. Just what I always wanted, the freedom to make my own place in life. He thought of his father and his oft-repeated counsel, "With every privilege comes responsibility. If you have the privilege of freedom, you have the responsibility of making that freedom meaningful and preserving that freedom for yourself and others as well."

CHAPTER TWO
SLAVES

HARK HAD BEEN A FRIEND AND CONFIDANT OF NAT TURNER, THE leader of the slave rebellion in Southampton County, Virginia. Although he had no active part in the deaths of sixty men, women and children, Hark and his family were among the thirty plus slaves that were sold "downriver" to be removed from Virginia. A well-to-do farmer, Grey James Thomas, from Cape Girardeau, Missouri, had been visiting his brother-in-law in Virginia at the time of the rebellion and the subsequent put-down of that uprising of both enslaved and free blacks. When the militia rendered their decision, eighteen of the insurrectionists were hanged, fifteen were acquitted and many others sold "downriver" to rid Virginia of their influence. Grey had taken advantage of the forced sale and bought the entire family at a considerable discount.

They traveled by wagon across Kentucky to Louisville, where their new owner, Grey Thomas, hired them to work on the side-wheeler steamboat, *Tecumseh*, to earn their passage downriver. At the little settlement of Cairo, Illinois, they left the *Tecumseh* and gained passage on the *Enterprise*, still working their way to Cape Girardeau. After arriving at the home place of Thomas, they were put to work, as a family, in the palatial home of the farm owner. Hark served as butler and valet, his wife, Sarah, cooked and cleaned, and the children, Joseph and Elizabeth, were houseboy and maid. Hark had shown himself as an intelligent and diligent worker, and when Grey Thomas discovered Hark could read and do numbers, he added the task of bookkeeper to his many other duties. It was unusual for a slave to know how to read for in many states it was illegal to educate the blacks, but Hark and Sarah had been houseworkers before and learned to read alongside their charges, the master's children. They passed that knowledge on to their children as well.

For over a decade, slavery had been a hotly debated issue in Missouri. With the passage of the Missouri Compromise in 1820 that prohibited slavery north of the 36°30' parallel, excluding Missouri, there were many residents that opposed slavery in Missouri even though it was allowed by the compromise. Grey Thomas had struggled with the issue, being a long-time slave owner who used them to build his sizable and productive farm, but his wife had often questioned the conscionable issue. After his wife died, he felt haunted by her repeated pleas to free the slaves. So Hark and his family had become almost like family in his home. Hark's wife, Sarah, reminded Grey of his departed wife in many ways, not the least of which was the many favorite dishes she cooked for him. After almost two years with Hark's family in his home, Grey had reached a decision.

"Hark, would you come into the office for a moment?" directed Grey.

"Yassuh, as you wish suh," responded the big man. Hark looked more the part of a field hand than a house-worker, standing just shy of six feet with broad muscled shoulders supporting a thick neck. His hair showed a few streaks of gray, and wrinkles marred his once handsome face, but his eyes flashed intelligence and kindness.

"Have a seat, Hark," motioned Grey as he seated himself behind the large oak desk.

Hark looked askance at his master, but when Grey motioned again, he took a seat in the arm chair beside the roll-top desk. Grey leaned back and looked at the man that had become more than property, but a friend and helper. He let a slow smile cross his face as he began to explain.

"Hark, I'm going into town and talk to my attorney, Johnathan Evans, and I'm going to have him draw up the papers for you and your family's manumission."

Hark's brow crinkled showing his question and he slowly asked, "Manumission? Do that mean . . .?"

"Yes, Hark. Manumission means I'll be granting you and your family your freedom. But, I would like you to stay on the farm and continue to work for me. And I'll pay each of you a regular wage, and maybe you could even build a home for your family here on the farm."

"Oh, Massuh Thomas, I . . . I . . . I don' know whut to say, suh. That be a wonderful thing you do. Freedom, oh my, I never thought . . ." stuttered the big slave as he looked at Grey with wide eyed wonder.

"And there's something else, Hark, I would be honored if you would take my last name as your own."

"Suh?"

"Well, you and your family don't have a last name, and I would like it if you would take Thomas as your last name," explained Grey.

"Oh, oh, yassuh, uh . . . " he dropped his head, slowly shaking it and lifted up his eyes, "Hark Thomas, Sarah Thomas, Joseph Thomas and Elizabeth Thomas, my oh my, that do sound good, suh, yassuh, it do." He grinned at his master and nodded his head as he asked, "Is that all suh? I'd shorely love to tell muh fam'ly, iffn' that be alright, suh?"

Grey grinned and said, "Of course, Hark. And could you have Joseph get my horse and buggy ready?"

Hark nodded his head as he stood, anxious to tell his wife the news of their coming freedom, and backed out of the office hurriedly.

Choosing to tell his wife first, Hark sent Joseph to get the buggy for Mr. Thomas, and drew his wife aside. Grey watched from the kitchen doorway as Hark and Sarah hugged one another and chattered on like excited school children. He grinned and returned to his office to retrieve the necessary paperwork for his journey to his attorney's office and the business he needed to conclude.

When Joseph returned to the house, Hark and Sarah with Elizabeth seated at the kitchen table, looked at the young man, resembling his father in looks and build, and asked him to be seated with his sister. As the two, Joseph, nearing sixteen, and Elizabeth, nearing fourteen, looked at their parents, Hark and Sarah couldn't contain their excitement and began talking together, but Sarah nodded to her husband and Hark said, "Children, we be gonna be free!" he announced.

Joseph and Elizabeth, or Lizzie as she preferred, looked at one another and back at their parents, not understanding what their father had said and Joseph asked, "Free? Whatchu mean, Pap?"

"Massuh Thomas is goin' to town to his 'torney, and makin' up the man . . uh . . . manumission papers to make us free!"

"You mean we ain't gonna be slaves no mo'?" asked Joseph as Lizzie nodded her head in agreement with his question.

"Tha's right boy, we ain't gonna be slaves no mo'!"

"But, but, what we gonna do? How we gonna live?" asked Joseph, almost afraid of the answer.

"Tha's da bes' part! We can stay ri'chere' and continue to do what we been doin' onliest, now we gonna be paid," as he motioned to each one of the family, "All us, gonna be paid. An' we can build us a home here on da farm," announced Hark, grinning and squeezing the hand of his excited wife. He then grabbed her around the waist, lifted her up and setting her back on her feet, the two began to dance around in a tight circle, laughing and giggling.

Joseph and Lizzie jumped up and mimicked their parents, and the four ended in a group hug, laughing and praising their Lord. Sarah said, "Husband, you should lead us in thankin' the Lawd for his mi'r-cle!" Hark looked at his wife and children and they stepped back, joined hands in a circle and Hark led the family in a prayer of thanksgiving.

At his "amen" the family resumed their excited chatter as the realization of their coming freedom filled them with a previously unexperienced joy and happiness. They returned to their daily duties throughout the house and grounds, but each one was heard singing or humming happy tunes. and none could stop smiling as they pondered their future of freedom.

Late afternoon, and after several trips to the fence to look down the road, Joseph shouted to the house, "Buggy's comin'!" and ran back to resume his vigil. He watched as the buggy neared, recognized it was not Grey Thomas' buggy but another familiar one that had visited the house often. It was Johnathan Evans, the attorney for Mr. Thomas. Mr. Evans spotted Joseph, he motioned for the young man to join him in the buggy when he stopped at the entry to the farm driveway. Joseph compiled and looked at Mr. Evans and said, "We was waitin' fo' massuh Thomas, he s'posed to be seein' you, suh."

"Yes, Joseph, Mr. Thomas was coming to see me, but I'm afraid I've got news for your family. Just wait till we get to the house and I'll tell you all, together."

It took only a moment for the buggy to pull up in front of the house and Hark, Sarah and Lizzie waited on the walkway. Their faces reflected confusion and concern at not seeing Mr. Thomas. The attorney stepped down from the buggy and suggested they all go inside before discussing anything and he led the way, with the entire family following.

Once inside, they seated themselves around the main table and Mr. Evans took the seat at the head, sat his leather case on the table top and began, "First, I'm afraid I have bad news for you," and looked around at the concerned faces and continued, "it seems that when Mr. Thomas was on his way into town, something, maybe a deer or fox or something, spooked his horse and the buggy careened off the road, and into the ditch. He was found by old Mr. Hawkens when he was riding into town. The doctor said Mr. Thomas broke his neck and suffered a dreadful concussion and probably died immediately."

Upon hearing the report, Sarah's hand flew to her mouth as she gasped, and the other one clasped the hand of her husband. The family looked at one another and Hark nodded to the attorney to continue.

"Mr. Thomas's death presents us with quite a dilemma. He had asked me to prepare manumission papers for you and your family," nodding to Hark, "but because he didn't get into my office to sign them, they are worthless." His shoulders raised, and he let a long breath escape as he looked at the different expectant faces staring at him.

"Now, I know he wanted you to be free, but, since he had no other family, when someone dies without family or a will showing anything different, all his property reverts to the state."

"But, he wanted us to be free," pleaded Hark, "cain't nuthin' be done?"

"No, I'm sorry Hark. That's just the law, and with the problems concerning slavery in the state of Missouri, what will happen is all of Mr. Thomas' property, you included, will be auctioned off to the highest bidder to settle the estate."

What had been expressions of joy just moments before, were now replaced with looks of fear as each of the family members looked at one another and back to the attorney, hoping for some other means to find freedom would be given by the man.

"What will be even worse, if it comes to the auction, your family probably would be split up and taken in different directions."

"No, no, no! Oh, lawdy, please no!" declared Sarah as she reached for the hands of her children.

"I can't let that happen, mistuh Evans, ain't dere nuthin' can be done?" pleaded Hark.

The attorney looked around the table and at Hark before he began, "What I'm about to say, I will never say again, and if you tell anyone I said this, I will deny it and call you a liar!" he admonished as he looked sternly at Hark.

"I unnerstan' suh," replied Hark, nodding his head for the attorney to continue.

"If I were you, I would do what Mr. Thomas would have wanted for you. I would pack up my family, take what I needed, and leave. The same Missouri Compromise law that made Missouri a slave state, also made slavery in the unorganized territories illegal. If I could get my family to the territories and away from slavery, I would not let anything or anyone stop me."

The attorney stood, picked up his satchel, and started to turn, hesitated and added, "It will be a few days before anyone comes to the farm to prepare for the auction and they can only sell what they find, and no one will know what was here before they came." Then he dropped his eyes and turned away from them and left the house. Hark and his family sat silent as they listened to the sounds of the buggy leaving the driveway. He looked at his wife and children and said, "We must be agoin'. It's gonna be a long trip and hard fo' each of us, but I don't sees how we have any choice."

Sarah nodded agreement with her husband and both looked at Joseph and Lizzie, who stared at their parents, waiting for instructions. Hark said, "Joseph, you go fetch them two bay mules, you know the ones, they's a pair and work good together. Hitch 'em up to the wagon and bring the wagon 'roun' back. Don't wan' none o' the others knowin' what we be doin' now, go on wid'chu." Joseph rose to follow his father's instructions as Hark turned to his wife and daughter. Lizzie was tasked with gathering the needed clothing, Sarah with the food and cooking gear, and he said he would be getting the other needed things. He stood and turned to his womenfolk and said, "We be leavin' just after dark, so we needs ta' hurry, now."

CHAPTER THREE
HOME

THE LODGEPOLE PINE GREW TALL, THIN AND STRAIGHT AND WERE SO close together it was difficult to make a way through them. Tatum began cutting a short distance into the grove and struggled with freeing the downed trees from entanglement with the others. Whenever he dropped a tree, upon falling the thick branches at the top would enmesh themselves with the dense growth of the still standing trees, and would have to be pulled down and free. After a considerable time of frustration at the entanglement of trees, he determined to cut as close to the edge of the thicket as possible. As he hacked away with his axe, the sounds echoed from the mountainside and each chop seemed to announce his presence. He worked as quickly as he could, using his tomahawk to trim each pole with a minimum of noise, and soon bundled seven of the skinny logs together for dragging to his homesite.

He searched for any giveaways that would tell of any visitors, and seeing none, he began the descent with the logs. The rocky hillside hindered him at every step, and his horse labored at the pull, often kicking stones free to tumble down the mountainside and crash into the aspen below. Tatum thought it would be a wonder if all his efforts at silence kept him from being discovered by any of his neighbors; the

Ute, Comanche or Apache. But he had to get his cabin built before winter set in, and sound or no sound, snow was coming. He debated with himself, thinking it would be better to spend more days on the erecting of the cabin before resuming his gathering of the lodgepole for the roof. After all, he could lay the logs much more quietly than chopping the lodgepole on the high ridges. He convinced himself of the wisdom of his thoughts and decided the next few days would be spent raising the walls.

Tatum had no sooner made the decision as he traversed the trail downslope, when a slight clearing in the black timber showed movement causing the big bay to stop with head raised and ears forward. The horse immediately showed fear, trembling and backstepping as Tatum tried to soothe the animal by stroking his neck as he looked down the trail to see the cause. What he saw made him grab for his Hawken, slung across his back, and pull it forward as he dropped into a crouch. He quickly checked to ensure the nipple held a fresh cap, and cocking the hammer he lifted the .54 caliber rifle to his shoulder. The monster on the trail rose to stand on its hind feet and let loose a roar that reverberated off the nearby pines and made Tatum think he could even smell the breath of the big Grizzly. The bear paddled his front feet as if fending off an unseen opponent and cocked its head side to side to see what threatened on the trail. With both horse and man now stilled, but trembling, the bear let another roar bellow, dropped to all fours and padded off into the trees on the downhill side.

Tatum didn't move, scanning the trees below, searching for any movement that would betray a charging bear, but he saw nothing. The big bay nervously watched the trees and the trail, prancing in place, anxious to be somewhere else. Tatum waited, watched, and listened, hearing nothing but the gentle whisper of the breeze through the pine boughs and seeing nothing but the quaking of the aspen leaves. He dared to take a breath, slowly stood and reached a comforting hand to the neck of the bay as he spoke softly to his four-legged friend. "Well, boy, thanks for the warning. Just when I was worried about being found out by Injuns, somethin' worse shows up, wouldn't ya know."

He cradled the rifle in his arm and grabbed the lead rope, still watching the trees below, and started out on the trail again with a relieved horse in tow. Within the hour they arrived at the homesite and loosed the bundle of logs. Tatum walked to the makeshift corral of branches, pushed his way in and haltered the sorrel. Leading his saddled horse from the corral, he grabbed the lead of the bay and walked the horses to the secondary clearing for the animals to graze. He picketed them securely and returned to the homesite to start his preparations for erecting the walls, no easy task for a man alone.

AFTER TWO WEEKS OF MEASURING, cutting, hacking, notching, dragging, pulling, and working himself and his horses beyond good judgment, Tatum stood back and admired his work. His cabin protruded from the cliff face as if it were an outgrowth or some deformity, but he was proud of his skeleton of a cabin. The two sidewalls, each with small window openings, were backed flush up against the cliff face and the front wall sported a window and a door. The three-sided structure was about twenty-foot square and the peaked side walls supported a cross beam that stretched from wall to wall. But there was no roof. The previously harvested lodgepoles had been used to improve the corral for the horses, and three of the poles had been converted into a much-needed travois to be used to transport the sod and moss for chinking and the winter's supply of meat. As Tatum surveyed his handiwork he remembered when he and his father had built the workshop at their last home and how his father had cautioned him, "Son, when you undertake a job, do it so you can take pride in it. Always do your best and that good work will be praise enough." Tatum nodded his head, satisfied he had done a good job, but it wasn't finished yet and it would be at least another week before he could call this a home.

He looked at the sun, calculated he still had time, and went to the corral for the sorrel. There would be time yet that he could cut and trim at least one trip's load of lodgepole. This time he brought the Johnson Cast-steel saw to do his work with a minimum of noise. He soon had a bundle of seven of the skinny logs and started back down the trail. By dusk, he came to his homesite, dropped the logs and returned his horse to the corral. He looked to the tree that held the deer carcass and cut the backstrap from the bone and skewered it to cook over the fire. As it began to sizzle and drip its juices, he poured himself a cup of warmed up coffee and moved the frying pan with the rest of the cornbread, slices of Indian potato, and onions closer to the flames. He had put in another full day and his appetite demanded satisfaction. He grinned to himself as he remembered the confrontation with the Grizzly on the trail over two weeks ago and thought to himself how glad he was it seemed to have left the area. As he looked at his dinner fare he said, "There ain't 'nuff here for me and no Grizz, that's for sure."

"Would you share your meal with us?" came a question from the trees that startled Tatum, causing him to jump to his feet and pivot around as he drew the Paterson from his holster. He dropped into a crouch as he searched the trees for the voice. He heard a slight giggle and another question, "Do you always welcome friends in this manner?" White Feather and her brother Raven stepped from behind the trees and walked into the clearing to join Tatum at the fire. Tatum relaxed when he recognized his friends from the Comanche, re-holstered his Colt and motioned for them to be seated.

"It is good to see you, but what brings you to my home?" asked Tatum. He knew the Comanche usually made their camp farther South in the Sangre's, but their hunting forays occasionally brought them North into the San Luis valley. His friendship with the Comanche came from his time fighting the smallpox outbreak that came from their captive white women taken from a wagon train. Tatum had warned the Comanche, helped them stay the plague and earned their friendship. White Feather had served as his interpreter and teacher of the Comanche language.

"We knew you were here, our warriors have watched and knew when you returned. We are with a hunting party and decided to visit," explained White Feather. Although she was a few summers older than Tatum, the two had felt an attraction to one another and Tatum was pleased to see the woman again.

He looked at Raven and asked, "Are you leading the hunters?" The man responded, "Yes, we are trailing a herd of buffalo and will probably catch up with them tomorrow."

"Well, this ain't no buffalo hump, but it's what I have and it is good to be able to share it with you, my friends." He walked to his pack and brought out two more tin plates and offered them to his visitors. He picked up the skewer with the back strap and extended it to Raven for him to cut a portion, then to White Feather, and took the remainder for himself. He did the same with the frying pan with the cornbread and vegetables, and set the pan aside, seated himself and the three ate for a few moments in silence. White Feather looked up at Tatum, smiled, and said, "You are building a home here, that is good."

Tatum looked at her, back at his cabin, and said, "Yeah, I've got more work to do, but it's coming along. Hopefully, I'll get it done before winter sets in."

Raven said, "This is country that many Ute come to hunt."

"Yeah, I've seen a couple bunches of 'em, but I don't think they know I'm here."

"If we know, they know," he stated bluntly.

It was a simple warning and one that Tatum knew he should heed, but he was also determined to make his home here. He asked Raven, "Do you think I can make peace with 'em?"

"They are not to be trusted," he declared.

Tatum knew the Comanche and Ute had been enemies, but Carson had explained that the Ute were known to be peaceful, but a wise man would be sparing with his trust.

"That's good to know. I've been tryin' to be careful, course you two snuck up on me. But I'll be more careful from here on out. I'd hate to go to all this work and have the Ute lift my hair and burn my cabin."

"Would you like to go with us on our hunt tomorrow?" asked White Feather, hopefully.

Tatum looked at her and smiled and answered, "Why, that'd be right nice. I'd like to hunt with you and some buffler steak would be a good change."

She smiled at his response and turned back to her eating, looked up at him again and smiled. He grinned at her and thought it would be nice to have some company for a change.

CHAPTER FOUR
HUNT

W<small>HITE</small> F<small>EATHER</small> <small>WAITED NEAR THE HORSES AS</small> T<small>ATUM</small> <small>ARRIVED TO</small> join the hunt. It was barely light with the sun still hidden behind the spine of the Sangre De Cristo. The hunting party was sequestered in the timber that trailed from the granite ridges of the mountains north of Tatum's cabin. He had chosen his site to overlook the broad expanse of sand dunes but be near the stream that circumvented the sandy hills. It was a short ride to the camp of the Comanche, and Tatum was pleased when he saw White Feather. He trailed the big bay that was encumbered with the empty travois, in hopes of bagging a buffalo for his own. He planned on leaving the pack animal at the camp with other mounts.

He reined up and dropped down from his sorrel, welcoming White Feather with a smile and a "Greetings my friend." She smiled back and drew near as she explained, "They are ready to start the pursuit," and turned to point, "the herd has followed the stream in the flats, there, and we approach from behind the tall willows at the stream edge."

White Feather was a proven warrior and hunter and would be a part of the hunt. It was not often a woman would be included among a hunting party, but White Feather was also a leader and daughter of the chief. Raven saw Tatum and walked toward the two, "We are ready, if you are to come with us," he directed.

Tatum mounted up and waited for White Feather to secure her horse and join him. The party was led by Raven as he rode off away from the trees. Buffalo were not as skittish as deer or elk, trusting in their bulk and the strength of their herd. They paid little attention to the approaching riders, who were mostly shielded from view by the tall wispy willows. Although some of the cows pushed the orange coated yearlings toward their herd as a precaution. A few of the bulls walked to the edge of the mass of brown, to watch and protect. It was not a massive herd, Tatum guessed the number at two hundred plus, but was sizeable enough that the hunters would be well rewarded. Tatum looked at the hunting party, noting only a few had rifles and those were trade fusils, almost useless against bulky beasts. As he looked, he counted twenty-two, including himself and White Feather. One other woman hunter was with the group, but she stayed close to Raven.Tatum guessed she was more concerned with the man than the beasts.

Raven stopped and motioned for several of the hunters to come forward for direction, including Tatum. As they drew near, he began, speaking softly, "You," motioning to a warrior near Tatum, "Dark Wolf, take Big Belly and two others, and go to the far side of the stream beyond the herd. You will be the last of the hunters as the herd tires, you will take your kill." He turned to another warrior and said, "Tall Elk, you and the others with rifles will go with Longbow to where the stream from the mountains joins this one, and place yourselves to use your rifles as the herd begins to move. The rest will come with me and we will take them from the flank and start our charge." Each one of the chosen leaders nodded to Raven and left to their assignments. Tatum looked back at White Feather, who nodded and mouthed the words, "Good Hunting," as he left.

He chose an embankment that rose from the creek bottom and stationed the other shooters, three in all, in a line so they would each have a clear field of fire and be to his left, placing himself last. They could see the woolies some three hundred yards to the south with several still lying down, unconcerned with the movement around them. Others were grazing in the dim early light and moving slowly with the waving of the tall grass in the breeze. Suddenly, as one, the herd jumped into motion and burly heads turned toward the upper end of the valley. The thunder of hooves drowned out the screams of the pursuing hunters. The dust from the flats rose in a billowing cloud, but Tatum could see the hunters, riding low on the necks of their ponies, gripping tightly with their legs, as hands drew back arrows to launch at the fleeing beasts. A few of the hunters held to the manes of their horses, thrusting their lances into the sides of their chosen target. Tatum searched but could not gain sight of White Feather. The thundering mass of brown was nearing the shooters and Tatum cautioned, "Wait for a good shot!" and realized he spoke in English and his fellow shooters probably didn't understand. He knew some Comanche or Shoshonean, but he just shook his head at his excited outburst and hunkered down to await his own shot.

He watched as the first of the herd neared, a young bull and waited to see if one of the others would choose it. He heard two of them take a shot but saw no result. He cocked the hammer and set the rear trigger, careful to line the front blade with the rear buckhorn sight he followed his target, took a breath and let some out and carefully squeezed as the muzzle followed his target. He saw a puff of dust from its lower chest and a stumble as the bull's head dropped and staggered. Within a few more steps, the bull's head dropped to the ground, the chin plowed a furrow in the fine alkaline dust as the front knees buckled and the carcass slid to a stop.

Tatum quickly brought his rifle down and began reloading, keeping his eyes on the passing herd, the other shooters also scrambling to reload. He placed a new cap on the nipple and cocked the hammer as he brought his rifle back to his shoulder. He set the rear trigger and took sight on another brown wooly but noticed an orange coated yearling struggling to keep up and he swung his sight to another. He started to squeeze off his shot but was stopped when he heard a shout from the shooter to his left. Between the embankment and the herd, he caught sight of a hunter just as the horse buckled, its front leg in a prairie dog hole causing the hunter catapult over the horse's head to land sprawled next to a clump of rabbit brush. The herd continued its flight and Tatum saw the hunter lay unmoving, perilously close to the stampeding. He swung the muzzle of his rifle in the direction of the downed hunter, to shoot anything that came near, but any shot would not immediately stop a runaway buffalo. Tatum jumped to his feet and ran to the hunter, thinking to drag him to safety while the others watched, ready to shoot any charging animal. His long strides quickly brought him to the hunter's side and he reached down with his free hand to grab the buckskin collar, suddenly realizing the hunter was White Feather. His hesitation was brief as he turned to drag the woman to safety, dropping over the embankment with his cargo, more concerned about safety than treatment.

Tatum dropped to his knees, looked at the unconscious woman, noted a twisted and obviously broken leg, and turned back to face the herd. He dropped two more buffalo before the last of the herd passed by and only then did he turn to see about White Feather. He leaned his rifle against the embankment and looked at the woman sprawled and unconscious at his feet. He pulled her to where her head was on the uphill side of the bank, carefully straightening her legs. The pain of the movement elicited a moan from the woman causing Tatum to show extra care with the obviously broken one. He rose and went to the creek as he undid his neckerchief, dipped it in the water, wrung it out and returned to wipe the face of the woman to try to rouse her. The cool cloth accomplished this, and her eyes fluttered open, surprised to see the face of Tatum before her. She looked quickly around, and asked, "My horse?"

Tatum shook his head at her question and asked, "How 'bout you? Anything besides your leg hurt?" She looked at him with a question on her face, then down at her leg. Her eyes widened, and she looked back at Tatum and said, "That does not look good."

Tatum chuckled at her remark and said, "If we leave it like that, you would sure walk funny."

She grinned at him and said, "I think it is starting to hurt now. What will you do?"

Before Tatum could answer, he was startled by the sudden arrival of Raven. He dropped from his horse at the sight of his sister lying on the ground. Tatum motioned to her leg and he looked at White Feather askance and she said, "My horse found a prairie dog hole and threw me over his head. Longbow brought me here." Raven looked at Tatum and said, "Can you do this?" motioning to her leg.

"I've never done it afore, but I reckon I can do it. But if you want to, have at it."

Raven looked at the other shooters and began barking orders, sending one to cut several willows for a splint, the other to hold White Feather along with Tatum. Raven grabbed a knife sheath from his belt and handed it to her, motioning for her to bite. She accepted it and shuffled herself farther up the embankment to a sitting position and her hands to the ground beside her to brace for the pain She nodded to her brother. He looked at the others and carefully grasped her ankle and foot, looked at his sister and stretched out his legs alongside to support hers and began to pull and maneuver the broken and twisted leg into place. White Feather let out a muffled scream and lost consciousness. Raven checked the alignment and placement of the bone, nodded his head in satisfaction, and motioned for Tatum to apply the willows branches for a splint.

"You will get your horse with the travois and take her to your cabin. We will butcher the kills and bring yours."

"Uh, I dropped three, but I only need one. Your people are welcome to the others, but I would like one of the hides."

Raven nodded his head and walked to his horse. With one glance back to his unconscious sister, he reined around to direct his party of hunters. Tatum crossed the creek to his tethered sorrel, mounted up and rode off to retrieve the bay and the travois. As he rode he began to wonder, *What am I gonna do with a woman at my cabin? Maybe they'll take her back to their camp, but she won't be able to ride. And I've got a lot more work to do before my cabin is even a cabin! Women!*

When he returned, White Feather was conscious, though in considerable pain and chewing on a small willow twig. Tatum knew the willow contained some pain killing element and White Feather probably could school him on other natural remedies. He grinned at her as she looked up at him and asked, "Why did you leave your horse across the creek?"

"I didn't want to drag you through the water on the travois, so I thought I'd just carry you over there," he explained as he bent down to pick her up. She winced as he lifted her, but the willow splint kept her leg straight and protected. After he crossed the shallow creek, he carefully lay her on the travois and covered her with a blanket and cautioned, "I think this might be a little bumpy, but I'll do my best to go as easy as I can." She nodded and forced a smile. He mounted up, grabbed the lead of the bay and started back.

Although it had been a busy morning, it was just midday when Tatum rode into the clearing with his cabin. He had been camped under a trio of tall ponderosa as he worked. He led the bay as close to his bedroll as possible. White Feather again forced a smile and looked up at him as he bent to pick her up and lay her on his bedroll. He tried his best to make her comfortable and asked, "What can I get for you? Or, what do you need me to do?"

She grinned and replied, "Nothing, I will be alright. You do what you must."

CHAPTER FIVE
FLIGHT

FIVE WEEKS. FIVE WEEKS OF LONG HARD TRAVEL, ALWAYS MOVING AT night, hiding during the day, taking their rest in thickets and groves, anywhere to keep from being spotted. They were fugitives, but from what or whom they did not know. With a lifetime of slavery, now on their own and without help of any kind, the Thomas family of four continued their flight from the farm in Missouri. Having their brief hope of freedom snatched suddenly from by the death of their master and owner, Grey Thomas, their choice to flee had driven them deeper into the unorganized territories. Hark knew slavery was against the law in the territories, but he could not bring himself to trust anyone and so drove his family to put as many miles behind them as possible. His hope was to distance them from their previous life of slavery and all the memories of that life

On their first night of travel he instructed his family on their route, "We just keep headin' west's all, see up thar," and pointed heavenward to the star-studded sky, "see that little constellation, the one with four stars kinda like a box?" He looked to his family as they gazed into the blackness, " looks like it's got a handle?" He saw heads nodding. "That's called the Wagon of Hea'bn, but some calls it the

Little Bear. Well if you look at the tongue of the wagon, or the tail of the bear," and was interrupted by his son.

"Pap, ain't no bears got tails!"

Hark chuckled at his son's remark and continued, "You right, boy. O.K. then, look at da tongue of the wagon an' see dat bright star?" Again, he was pleased at the nodding heads. "Wal, dat's da North Star, an' it's always to our North. So, if'n we just keep it off'n our right shoulder, we be headin' West to freedom!"

"Maybe we should call it our Freedom star then," declared Sarah as she turned and smiled at her husband.

"Tha's a good idee, we just do that. That be our Freedom Star!" he proclaimed.

Now, over five weeks later, the Freedom star was still off their left shoulder, but the way West wasn't any easier. The rain had started mid-afternoon and continued unabated. But as dusk put daylight to rest, Hark was determined to travel and slapped the reins on the rumps of the mules to start off again. They only got an occasional glimpse of the stars overhead, but Hark would use any distant land-mark, as the rain allowed, to keep up the pace.

It was nigh unto midnight and Hark pulled the wagon into a grove of trees to give the mules a short rest. The rain had let up, but the remnants dripped from the overhead branches. Hark found a spot of high ground with a tall white pine that offered some shelter and pulled the wagon under the long branches. Everyone climbed down, tried to shake the water from their hats and coats, and Sarah asked, "Could we start a fire to warm up a mite?"

Hark looked at his wife, feeling her discomfort and said, "Sugarplum, I don't think there's a dry piece of wood this side o' da Mississippi. Come on an' sit down nex' ta' me, I'll warm you up." He motioned for her to join him and leaned back against the rough bark of the tree. Joseph and Lizzie joined them. Lizzie said, "Pap, is this what they calls a fam'ly tree?" and giggled.

"Sho' nuff' girl, leastwise, it's our fam'ly tree."

Hark looked at his wife and began to sing,

"Climbin' up d' mountain, children
Didn't come here to stay
And if I nevermore see you again
Gonna meet you at de judgment day,"
His family joined him as they continued their song,
"Hebrew in de fiery furnace
And dey begin to pray
And de good Lawd smote dat fire out
Oh, wasn't dat a mighty day!
Good Lord, wasn't dat a mighty day!"

Sarah had a satchel with cornbread and passed it around for each one to have a little sustenance and Joseph said, "Pap, how 'bout lettin' me take the rifle out in da mornin' and get us some fresh meat, whatsay?"

"That might be alright boy, but we needs to wait till we see where we be come daylight."

"Ummhumm, I reckon," replied Joseph.

The clouds had cleared off and the stars twinkled their invitation for the travelers to resume their journey and Hark complied. Keeping to the roadway because of the moist soil, they made good time considering the storm. It was coming on morning light when they neared a river crossing and stopped. Hark looked to Joseph and said, "While that moon is still bright, how 'bout you take the rifle and such, and your sister, and wade 'cross that river. If it gits too deep, you bring her back, now, y'hear? Yore Mam and me'll follow soon's you git a'crost."

Joseph stretched his legs to the wagon hub and dropped to the ground. He reached up and took the rifle, powder-horn and possibles bag from his Pap, helped Lizzie to the ground and walked to the water's edge. The moonlight reflected off the passing water, but it appeared shallow and wasn't moving too fast, so he grasped Lizzie's hand in his and stepped in. He looked back at her and reassured her, "I'll take it easy, Lizzie, just hold on tight."

They were both barefoot and the water was cold, but tolerable. They felt their way along the sandy bottom, occasionally stubbing their toes on river donies, and the current tugging at their clothes. Joseph stayed to the upstream side to break the force of the current for his sister. As they neared the middle of the channel, the current was stronger, and the water was crotch deep on Joseph, approaching waist deep on Lizzie. He looked at his sister and she nodded her head for him to keep going and he cautiously stepped forward, feeling for any drop-offs or hazards. A few more steps and the water was to Joseph's waist and the ribs of Lizzie, but she pushed him on and within a few steps the river bottom was rising up for them. He held the rifle and makings over his head, and they soon made it to the shallows and onto the bank.

Lizzie sat down as Joseph waved back to his father, uncertain if his father could see him in the moonlight, he added a long whistle just in case. Joseph heard splashing of water and knew his father had goaded the mules into the stream. The heavier wagon dug its wheels deeper into the river bottom as they neared the middle of the channel and Hark slapped the reins to the rumps of the animals to encourage them to pull harder. Joseph heard a low roar coming from upstream and looked to see a foaming wall of water coming at a rush toward the wagon. He looked at his father and yelled in a panic, motioning and hollered, "Come on mules! Pull! Pap, there's water comin'! Hurry!" He saw his Pap stand in the wagon box in front of the spring seat and frantically slap the reins and shout threats to the mules. But before they could free the wagon from the sandy bottom, the huge foamy wave bore down upon them and they disappeared. Lizzie jumped to her feet and shouted, "Momma! Pap!" she turned to Joseph and asked, "Can't we do anything?" Joseph stood staring hopelessly at the water that carried trees and stumps and other debris in the flood that rushed past the two onlookers.

Joseph looked at his sister, grabbed her hand and shouted, "C'mon sis!" and started running along the bank of the mad river. They stopped and cupped hands to their mouths shouting, "Momma! Pap! Where are you!"Using the remains of the moonlight to guide them as they hoped against hope of finding their folks wading from the rushing stream. Again they stopped and shouted, but no answer came. It was early morning and full light when they saw the first mule struggling from the water, bits of harness trailing behind. Joseph spoke softly to the animal and reached out for the bridle to help pull it up the bank. The mule struggled, but with the encouragement from the man and the additional leverage, he pushed from the water and up the bank. Joseph handed the mule off to Lizzie and ran back to the bank to search both banks for any sign of the other mule or their folks. Seeing nothing, they continued downstream, stopping often to call for their parents, "Momma! Pap! Please answer! Lizzie was leading the mule and Joseph searched every jumble of debris and branch tangle at the river's edge.

A short while later, they spotted the second mule, standing with head down, well back from the river and sucking wind like he was having trouble getting air. As they approached he lifted his head and Joseph would have sworn the mule smiled at him as he let out a bray. He walked up to the animal and hugged his neck and asked, "Well, boy, it's good to see you but where's the folks?" As he stood by the mule he searched the river bank for any other sign. He started to turn away when a patch of color caught his eye. He handed the lead for the mule to his sister and said, "Wait here, I'll be right back, gotta check on sumpin'."

He walked to the edge of the river that made a bend and spotted a tangle of driftwood washed against the bank and under an overhang of branches from an old cottonwood. He knelt down at the edge of the bank and recognized the cloth of his mother's dress. He looked back at Lizzie and stepped off the bank and into the water. He struggled with the many branches and the current, still strong though waning, and tried to free what he recognized as his mother's body. He grabbed a large branch and fought against the current, freed the branch and let it go with the water. He gasped as he spotted his father's body, arms wrapped around his mother. Their bodies bobbed in the water until Joseph freed his mother and dragged her to the bank. He returned for his father, and fought the remaining tangle to free them. He struggled to see through the tears as he dragged his father's body to the grassy bank to lay it next to his mother's. He dropped to his knees beside them, sucking for air in his exhaustion, fighting back tears. He looked to his sister, also on her knees, head bowed and sobbing, yet holding tight to the leads of the two mules.

"HERE'S A BAG OF SMOKED MEAT IF YOU GET HUNGRY AND HERE'S A canteen of water. The best thing you can do is get some rest while I'm gone," said Tatum as he knelt next to White Feather. She lay on his bedroll under the towering ponderosa with a thick cushion of the long pine needles under the ground cover. A rolled-up blanket under her head for a pillow, she still looked uncomfortable, but with the broken leg wrapped tightly, she was as comfortable as she could be.

She smiled at Tatum and replied, "You do what you must, I will rest fine right here."

"Well, Raven should be along any time now. He said he'd bring my buffalo meat and hide, so if I'm not back by then, you just take it easy and let that leg heal," he admonished. She nodded her head in understanding, winced a little as she tried to arrange herself for more comfort, and waved him away. He stood and went to the tethered horses to resume the work of retrieving more lodgepole pine for the roof of his cabin. The travois had been dropped beside the corral and was replaced by a pack-saddle and additional coils of hemp rope. This trip he planned on using both horses.

He made short work of dropping another fourteen poles with the saw. And using his tomahawk with the metal blade he quickly trimmed each of the poles. He made two bundles of seven poles each and secured one behind each horse to snake from the trees and back to the cabin. As he led the sorrel, the lead rope of the bay tied to the bundle of the sorrel, he saw the many trips on the trail were leaving marks. When snaking the larger logs from the black timber, he seldom used the same trail, but the lodgepole pine grew closer together and proved impossible to do random cuts.

Well, guess I'm gonna have to hurry up and get all I need so I can cover up the trail sooner. Course, it is higher up the mountains and won't be easily seen, but still . . . he thought as he trudged along the trail. *I'm also gonna have to make some rack for holding the meat in the cave, but I can use a few of these logs for that, I reckon.* He looked back at the trail before him as it led into the open and across an expanse of slide rock. The flat surfaced granite stone had gathered a thin layer of spotty green and orange moss, meaning footing was challenging, even though an ancient trail led across it.

Suddenly he was brought from his musings when a clatter of hooves startled him and the horses. A group of bighorn sheep, apparently spooked from below in the timber, bounded their way up the rock without a single misstep. Tatum froze in place as he watched five ewes, four lambs, and three rams, one with a full curl of his horns, clamor up the slide. He had seen bighorns from a distance, but never this close and he was awestruck at their confident climb. Even the lambs scampered over the uneven and unstable stones without hesitation. Only the big ram paused in his climb as he looked at Tatum, as if daring him to follow. When they flashed their dingy white rumps in good bye and disappeared in the rocks and aspen, Tatum resumed his trek back to camp.

He grinned to himself as he walked, thinking of all the experiences he'd had since leaving Missouri, and remembering the many times he and his father had sat at the table talking about one day going to the mountains. "Well, Pa, I sure wish you were here with me, but I'm certain you and Ma kinda like it where you are But that don't keep me from missin' you both!" he declared out loud, looking heavenward where he firmly believed his parents waited.

The work with the poles had consumed most of the afternoon and the journey back traced the dropping of the sun behind the far mountains. He had one last look at the broad strokes of orange and gold that painted the western sky before dropping into the last stretch of black timber nearing his camp. The twilight was ample for him to de-rig the horses and put them into the corral. He turned and started toward his camp by the trees and stopped abruptly when he was greeted by White Feather,

"I am glad you returned."

Tatum saw the pile of meat on the hide that lay nearby and the wrapped hide beside it, looked at White Feather and said, "I thought Raven was taking you back to your village."

"I cannot ride with this," motioning to her leg, "and I cannot take a travois that far." She smiled at his response, delighting in his quandary. "When I can ride, I will go back to my village. I will try not to be too much trouble, and I will help when I can."

"Uh . . . uh . . . yeah, . . . I guess." He stammered as he walked nearer. She had pushed herself up against the log by the fire ring, stifling a giggle.

"Well," he stuttered as he looked at the pile of meat, "I guess a buffalo steak would do us both a lot of good." He turned to the fire ring and gathered some kindling from the wood stack, put a small bit of tinder in the middle of the cleared away ashes, stacked the kindling over it and reached into his possibles bag for his flint and steel. Striking them, he soon had sparks on the tinder. He blew gently to get a flame and the tongue of orange licked at the kindle and caught. He stacked additional sticks and more for the fire then went to his panniers and dug around, retrieved a tin plate and walked back to the side of White Feather. He handed her the tin plate, slipped his Bowie from the sheath at his back and handed it to her and said, "How 'bout you cuttin' us a couple steaks while I get us some new willows to hang 'em on?" Without waiting for an answer, he went to the meat pile, grabbed a sizeable cut and handed it to White Feather. She smiled at him, nodded her head and watched as he headed to the stream below to retrieve the willows.

When he returned, he dropped some fresh sego lily roots and wild onions beside White Feather, retrieved the cut steaks and skewered them on the willows and hung them over the fire. He went to his packs, retrieved the coffee pot, a frying pan, a pot, and some corn flour and returned to the woman's side. Taking the canteen, he put water in the pot, sat it beside the fire, and motioned to White Feather and the vegetables and the corn flour, indicating the expected action. He stood with the canteen and the coffee pot and walked to the small stream that came from the cavern and filled both. When he returned to the fire, he placed the coffee pot on the flat stone near the flames, and sat back to watch White Feather struggle with the vegetables and the cornbread makings. He grinned at her and reached for the corn-bread makings and the frying pan and said, "I'll do that, you fix the vegetables." She nodded at him and did as instructed.

When everything was cooking, he sat back with arms folded across his chest and said, "You know, having company might not be too bad."

White Feather looked at him, let a bit of a giggle escape and said, "If I had known you were going to make me your captive, , I might have risked the ride back to my village!"

Tatum chuckled, "Some slave you'd make, you can't even get around."

They both laughed as the tension slipped away. Feather said, "This," motioning to her leg, "will not take too long to heal, but it will be difficult to move about for a while."

Tatum looked at her and grinned as he had a thought, "What you need is a crutch!"

"A crutch? What do you mean?"

"You know, a crutch, to help you walk around till that heals up," he said enthusiastically. "It's too late to find one now, but in the mornin' I'll look for what you need, and we'll fix you up a good crutch. It's like, well, a sapling with a fork in it. And you put the forked end under your arm and . . ." he looked at her confused expression and added, "Ah, it's too hard to explain. I'll just have to show you tomorrow." She nodded her head and they began dishing up their supper.

CHAPTER SEVEN
DISCOVERY

JOSEPH STRUGGLED WITH THE BODIES OF HIS MOTHER AND FATHER, seeking to find a suitable place for burial away from the river bed and back in the trees. Lizzie had been tasked with tending the mules, knowing she would be of little help with the burials. He found a place amidst a small cluster of birch and scratched away as much of the topsoil as he could with only a flat rock and a stick. He dragged the bodies into the depression, laid them side by side as respectfully as he could, fighting back tears as he worked. He straightened the remnants of his mother's dress, and as he pushed his father closer to his mother, he heard a slight jingle and paused. He looked at his father's body, saw a lump at his side, just below his belt, and he reached out and tugged at the belt and the lump. He retrieved a leather drawstring pouch, bigger than his hand, and sat back on his haunches as he opened the heavy sack. He looked into the dark pocket, eyes growing wide, as he emptied several gold coins into his hand. He lifted his head and looked around as if expecting someone to catch him. He rose to his knees and looked at the closed eyes of his Pap and whispered, "What did you do Pap? Where'd this money come from?"

He put the coins back in the pouch, tucked the pouch into his britches in a similar fashion as his father had carried it, and began covering the bodies with the loose soil. As he worked, his mind chased all kinds of thought. *He musta taken it from Massuh Thomas' house. Mebbe he was thinkin' the Massuh was gonna pay us anyway and he sure couldn't use it. It'll sho' he'p us make it to da West, if'n we can find some place to buy whut we needs, that is.* He knew the soil would not be enough to properly protect the bodies of his parents and began carrying stones for a grave cover.

When he finished, he went to Lizzie and said, "Let's tie the mules off, and you come on wid me and we'll say some words o'er the graves."

The young girl nodded her head, handed her brother the leads and waited while he tied them off to a nearby cottonwood sapling. The mules busied themselves with the tall grasses and seemed content. Joseph took Lizzie's hand and they walked to the graves. They stood silently for a moment and Joseph started reciting the twenty-third Psalm and Lizzie joined in at, "he leadeth me beside the still waters. He restoreth my soul: He leadeth me in the paths of righteousness for His name's sake." They continued reciting together and when they finished with, ". . . dwell in the house of the Lord forever."

Lizzie looked at her brother and said, "That's where they are now, aren't they?"

"Yes, Lizzie, they both be up there lookin' down on us now. So, we gots to get goin', just like we would if Pap was pushin' us on."

"But it's still daylight. Shouldn't we wait till dark?"

"Well, we needs da light to find us sumpin' to eat. Mebbe I can shoot us some meat and you can fin' us sumpin' like Momma used to do, you know, some a' dem plants like onions an' such?"

"Well, I can try, I s'pose," replied the fearful youngster.

They mounted the mules, Joseph had cut away the harness so the only rigging they had were the bridles and reins. He salvaged most of the harness, thinking they might have a need farther along, and also cut the reins, making one rein per animal suffice by converting them into a loop rein and saving the others for additional strapping. Joseph led out, trying to stay as near the tree line as possible for game, but still make time. Lizzie searched the grounds around them as they rode. But the uncertain days before them kept crowding into her mind and she finally gave voice when she asked simply, "What we gonna do, Joseph?"

"We're gonna get us sumpin' to eat, that's what. Keep lookin'!"

"That ain't what I meant. I mean what we gonna do about tomorrow and the next day and the next?"

"Well Lizzie, we left Missouri cuz we wanted to be free. An' that's still what we want, ain't it?"

"Yeah, but without Pap and Mam, what we gonna do?" she timidly asked.

"We gonna do the same thing as if Pap and Mam were still here. We goin' West. I heard tell of the mountains, and even beyond 'em, that there's lots a land for the takin', an' all we gots to do is find us a piece an' build us a home on it."

"How we gonna do that? You ain't never built no home afo'," she declared.

"Ain't nuthin' to it. Just put one stick together with 'nother un' and then do it again, an' purty soon, ya gots a home!"

"It cain't be dat easy, cuz ever'body'd be doin' it!"

"Didn't say twas easy. Gonna take a lot a work, but you n' me, we can do anythin' we sets our mind to! And don't ferget it!" declared Joseph as he twisted around to look at his little sister. As he turned back, he spotted movement near the willows by the creek below them and he reined up, twisting back to shush his sister and pointing toward the creek. A small spike buck had tiptoed to the water and lifted his head at the sound from the siblings. They were partially shielded behind a tall alder bush. The buck dropped his head again and Joseph slid off the mule, motioning Lizzie to move up and take the lead of his mount.

Placing the lead in her hand, he checked the rifle, used the small horn to put powder in the pan and dropped the frizen. He cocked the hammer, and stealthily moved to the edge of the alder, slowly dropped to one knee and brought the rifle to bear on the buck. He set the rear trigger, carefully took aim, and slowly squeezed the small front trigger. The hammer dropped and flint struck frizen, igniting the flash pan and the rifle bucked as the gray cloud and blast thundered from the muzzle.

Joseph quickly stood to see past the smoke and saw the buck stagger and fall. He shouted, "We got meat!" Lizzie clapped her hands and almost dropped the lead to the mule, that was now skittish after the roar of the rifle and the shouting of Joseph. Joseph, seeing the spooked animal, held out a hand and spoke soothingly to the mule who stared with wide eyes and ears forward trying to figure out what had happened. He stopped his side step, and Lizzie, with a tight grip on the rein and an arm stretched to its limit, motioned for Joseph to take the rein before she fell off her mule.

Joseph made short work of dressing out the deer, deboning all the usable meat and using the hide to make a bundle. Taking the straps from the reins, he made a tight bundle and used the larger harness to strap it on the haunches of the mule. He was whistling a combination of old tunes and Lizzie laughed at her brother and his antics as he reached under the flanks of the mule to secure the package. He stood with hands on hips and looked at his sister and said, "No laughin' now. We got meat to eat so we need to be findin' us a place back in the trees and fill our feed bag!"

"Who's cookin'? You or me? And don't you say you be doin' it, we both know better."

CHAPTER EIGHT
FALLS

THE HIGH-PITCHED SQUEAL DROPPED OFF TO A BUGLING WHISTLING sound that ended in three grunts. Tatum had never heard such a sound in the woods and stood frozen, listening. He was busy putting the finishing touches on the aspen sapling he was fashioning into a crutch for White Feather and he stopped his carving at the sound. With a questioning look on his face, he glanced over at the reclining woman. She saw his expression of wonder and slowly let a smile cross her face as she asked, "Have you not heard the bugle of the wapiti before?"

"Wapiti?"

"I think you white people call it an elk, a bull elk. He is gathering his herd of cows and is telling the other bulls to stay away or be prepared to fight!" she explained, adjusting herself to a more comfortable position on her blankets beside the gray log.

Before he could respond, the bull sounded the bugling call again followed by the clatter of antlers. To Tatum it sounded like the massive animal was charging through the timber and he looked again to White Feather.

"He is sharpening his antlers against a tree to prepare to do battle with another. The winner gets the herd and the loser spends a lonely winter," she added.

Tatum turned his attention back to his handiwork, the aspen sapling was becoming the crutch he envisioned for White Feather. The bark had been peeled, the fork was well padded with three rabbit pelts, and the protruding lower branch had been fashioned to a hand-hold. He stood it upright and looked at White Feather, "Let's see if this is gonna fit and work for you."

He walked to her side and he reached down for her arm to help her to her feet. She stood with one hand on his left shoulder as he demonstrated how to use the crutch with his right arm. He handed it to her and she put it under her left arm to take the weight from her injured leg. He saw her surprise at the comfort of the crutch and how easily she could use it.

After taking a couple of strides, she looked back at Tatum with a wide grin splitting her face as she said, "This is wonderful! I will be able to get around much easier! Thank you, my friend."

Tatum flashed a smile of approval and satisfaction and asked, "How is your leg feeling today?"

"I believe it is healing. It must be, it seems to itch all the time!"

"Well, how 'bout sittin' down and let me take a look. That splint could use some adjustin' I think."

As he unwrapped the leg, he noticed the wrinkling of the skin and knew it was from the poultice of alumroot and kinnikinnick. The swelling had subsided, and the splint had loosened. At White Feather's direction, he made and applied a poultice of dried alder leaves and sagebrush leaves. After wrapping her leg with the previously used cut-off portion of a blanket, he re-applied the willow branch splint and wrapped it with the rawhide thongs. She stood and tested her crutch again by hobbling to the edge of the clearing and back to the log. As she seated herself, she looked at Tatum, "You would make a good medicine man."

Tatum chuckled and said, "Oh yeah, that's what I want to do, spend my life with sick and injured folks, present company excluded, of course."

"I would like to go to the water. I have not bathed since I did this," she motioned toward her leg, "and I would like to, if you would help me."

"Help bathe you?! I can't do that! You're a woman!" exclaimed Tatum, flustered.

"No, not that. Just help me to the water," White Feather explained, giggling at his embarrassment.

"Oh, uh . . . yeah, I can do that. Say, I know a great place. Do you think you could ride a little way? Or would you rather use the travois?"

"If it is not too far, I could ride," she answered, wondering at his intended destination.

A SHORT WHILE later they were on their way along a south bound trail just inside the edge of the trees overlooking the wide expanse of the many sand dunes, and in the distance, the San Luis valley. The first part of the trail led them to climb the switch-back narrow path to the top of the ridge. It then dropped down and crossed the finger of sand that crawled toward the mountain top before they came to the wider valley that held the stream and trail that crossed the Sangre de Cristo mountain range. They continued along the southerly trail that wove in and out of the timber and the hillsides that held spotty clusters of pinyon, juniper and cedar.

It was nearing mid-day when Tatum reined up among a cluster of juniper nestled near a large stack of striated boulders. He stepped down, tethered his mount and walked to the big bay and helped White Feather to the ground. She fussed a little, getting her crutch situated under her arm. A small stream cascaded down the steeper rock-strewn hillside that was thick with twisted cedar and juniper. She looked at Tatum and said, "That's not a very big stream. I was hoping for a deep pool to swim in, or at least more water."

He grinned at her and said, "Just wait, there's a spot up here I think you will like. Come on, follow me." He started up a footpath beside the chattering stream, paused and waited for her to follow. As she neared, he said, "You go ahead, I'll follow, just in case you need some help getting up there."

Tatum watched as the trail rose and White Feather struggled, but valiantly pushed on with an occasional glimpse over her shoulder at Tatum. Whenever he caught her looking, he grinned and motioned her onward. He knew she could hear the roar and crashing of water and would wonder how such a small stream could make so much noise.

Suddenly, as the trail bent around a corner of a towering cliff, she saw the water falling from a height of twenty-five feet in a shower of white that splashed on the nearby crevasse walls into a small pool. She turned and looked at a broad smiling Tatum as he stepped beside her and said, "Whatchu think?"

"Oohh, it, it's beautiful!" she almost had to shout because of the cascading water.

Tatum motioned to a cut in the crevasse wall that served as a bench and said, "You'll need to leave your splint on, but you can sit here and take off your tunic and kinda scoot yourself into the pool." He handed her a small remnant of a bar of lye soap and said, "I'll put the blanket here on the rocks for you to dry off with. I'll be just below, so if you need help, just holler."

She used her own soap, made from the roots of the yucca and with a more pleasant odor than the lye, and before long, hobbled from the small pool to the waiting blanket. Refreshed and happy, she called to Tatum as she began descending the trail. His answering reply surprised her as it came from the trees at the edge of the trail. He stepped to her side and said, "Now, it's my turn. There's a log just yonder," motioning with a head nod, "that makes a purty good seat. I won't be long."

Upon his return from his wash, they went to the horses and Tatum took out some smoked venison from the saddle bags and the canteen of water. Seating themselves on a wide flat chunk of granite that had fallen from the cliff face eons ago, they enjoyed their brief interlude in the sun. As they ate, Tatum thought he saw movement on the slope of the ridge to their right. White Feather saw his gaze and looked in the same direction just in time to see the rumps of several bighorn sheep as they grazed the grass among the rocks. Several year-ling lambs scampered about, butting one another and jumping from rock to rock, showing their amazing agility. Tatum asked White Feather, "Are they good eating?"

She looked at him and smiled and said, "Yes, if the meat is prepared right. It is very good."

He nodded and walked to his sorrel, grabbed the longbow and quiver of arrows, and walked back to the seated White Feather. She had seen the unstrung longbow before and wondered at the size of it, but she had never seen him use it. He had chosen to leave his rifle behind, thinking if he saw any game, he would use the bow, always determined to make as little noise as possible.

She had seen the unstrung longbow before and wondered at the size of it, but she had never seen him use it. White Feather watched as he stepped across the lower limb of the bow, took the top limb in hand and bent it down to string the weapon. As she watched she said, "I have never seen a bow as tall as that, but you will have a hard time getting close enough to the bighorn. They have very good eyesight."

"Well, it's always worth a try. Care to come along?"

The sheep were about two hundred yards away when they started their approach. The hunters kept a cluster of juniper between them and as Tatum started to work around the cluster, White Feather whispered, "I'll wait here." Tatum nodded his understanding and in a crouch, worked a little closer to the hillside.

He watched the animals, noticing a large ram on the uphill side of the small herd, had spotted him. But the sheep were confident in their abilities to escape quickly over the jumble of boulders that make pursuit difficult, and they tarried, but watched as Tatum neared. When he was about eighty yards from them, he was careful not to look directly at them, but stayed partially shielded beside a squat pinyin. Setting his eyes on a young solitary ram, he stepped into his draw and let fly the long alder-wood arrow. The quick movement of the release startled the big ram, who brought his head up but remained immobile as the arrow whispered its way to impale itself deep into the chest of the ram. The bighorn jumped straight up and crumpled into a pile without any further movement. The rest of the herd scattered and scampered over the rocks with graceful bounds and topped the ridge to disappear beyond.

Tatum looked back at White Feather who stood with a bewildered look on her face as she hunched with her crutch , and shook her head as she asked, "How did you do that? That was . . . that was . . . I have never seen any warrior shoot an arrow that far and that . . . it dropped that ram as if you hit it with a club!" Her amazement clouded her face and she shook her head again.

"Wait there, I'll fetch the meat," he said, chuckling, as he started up the hillside to retrieve the carcass. By the time he had dressed out the carcass, he bent to pull the hide of meat onto his back and looked below to see White Feather seated on the big bay and holding the lead of the sorrel. He grinned and worked his way to her side with his burden of meat.*Maybe she can show me the right way to fix this sheep, so we can have a special meal tonight. It'll be a good change,* he thought as he negotiated the hillside.

HIS WORDS PROVED prophetic and he savored the tender meat, broiled over the open fire, and the vegetables collected from the banks of the stream below the cabin. It had been a pleasant day and he had enjoyed the company, especially for a solitary man that didn't like to be around people.

CHAPTER NINE
SUPPLIES

THE TRAIL JUST SOUTH OF THE RIVER RODE THE LOW RISING HILLS AND swales making the rocking gait of the mules hypnotic. Joseph and Lizzie ambled on in silence, with the few sounds of the prairie coming from scattered cicadas, bullfrogs in the backwaters of the winding river, and the gentle breeze rattling the few remaining leaves of the cottonwoods and alders. The shuffling hooves of the mules occasionally kicked a stone rolling and lifting small puffs of dust. The dry air clogged the mules nostrils and the dust from the trail added to their discomfort. Without a cloud in the sky, the sun beamed unhindered upon their backs and the mules. The leather harness held the heat and left soapy sweat beneath, adding to the stink of their travel.

With heavy eyelids and parched throat, Lizzie asked, "Joseph, can we stops at the river, get some shade an' mebbe wash up in the water? I's sizzlin' like frog legs in a fryin' pan."

Joseph started to turn to his sister and stopped the mule. He leaned right and left and shaded his eyes. He squinted his eyes and leaned forward as if the closer the lean the better the view, but the object of his gaze was just shy of half a mile away. When he didn't answer, Lizzie moved her mule up beside his and looked at her brother. She turned to look in the same direction as Joseph. She mimicked him by shading her eyes and leaning slightly forward and asked, "What is it?"

"I think it's a tradin' post or sumpin', don't rightly know. I hope it is, cuz we could use some supplies for we go any further."

"Supplies? How you gonna pay for supplies? You ain't got no money!"

"Ummhummm, shore do! Pa had some stashed in a pouch," he slapped the pouch at his waist for emphasis, "and I'm thinkin' it's 'nuff to get whut we need."

Lizzie dropped the hand from her eyes and twisted to look at her brother, "Whyn't you tell me you gots money? And how you gonna get stuff from white folks without them thinkin' you a runaway?"

"Don't make no difference. Don't you 'member Pap tellin' us slavery is outlawed in the territories?"

"Is we in da territories?" asked Lizzie with eyes wide.

"Yup! We is," retorted Joseph with a grin. He gigged his mule toward the river and the shade of the cottonwoods.

The river was a twisting, winding, slow rolling river that wound its way through the prairie flats of the Great Plains. With shallow waters, except during the spring runoff, it was an easy cross, but Joseph and Lizzie chose to rest their mules in the shade while they broiled some more deer steaks. Joseph wanted to ponder their next move a little more and to mentally make a list of their needs. He was certain the money in the pouch would be more than sufficient for securing their supplies and maybe even some additional gear.

While Joseph prepared the meat, Lizzie took a short walk along the river bank looking for anything that would supplement their meal. She had learned a lot from her mother during the first days of their journey and she scanned the water's edge for any familiar growths. She gathered some onions, a pocketful of raspberries, and a handful of strawberries. When she returned to the fire, the meat was ready, and she shared her bounty with her brother.

"I figger 'bout the only thing we can do is just ride right in as if we owned the place!" declared Joseph as he looked across the river, envisioning the trading post on the far side.

"Bof' of us?" asked a fearful Lizzie.

"Yup! Both of us, ride in together. Pap used to allus' say, 'If you act likes you knows whatchu doin', folk'sll just think you do!" He lifted his head to show more confidence than he had, nodded it, and looked at his sister with a wide grin.

Lizzie looked at her brother and stifled a laugh as she replied, "If you go lookin' like that, they'll think you et a mouse or sumpin'!"

"Well, come on an' eat. We needs to git on o'er there and git things 'fore dark comes. Don't wanna be caught in da' open wid no cover or nuthin'. But, after we gits our supplies, I'm thinkin' we'll go back to travelin' by the stars."

Both Joseph and Lizzie anxiously downed their food and readily broke camp for the short jaunt to the fort. They crossed the river, only knee deep to the mules, and moved up the opposite bank to the flats. A few scrub pinyon and clusters of sage grew between them and the fort and the enormous adobe structure surprised the two young travelers. They had never seen anything so massive. The towering walls, bastions, and huge gates were impressive, but what caught their attention was the number of tipis and wigwams arrayed outside of the fort and the hundreds of Indians wandering freely about. Joseph reined up and held a hand out for Lizzie to stop. They looked at one another, back at the fort and the many people, white and Indian alike, and back to each other. Joseph sucked in a deep breath that lifted his shoulders, grinned at his sister, and dug his heels into the mule's ribs.

Although Joseph was what his Pap called, 'full growed', his facial features betrayed his youth and Lizzie, at fourteen, was just a budding woman. The Indians, Cheyenne mostly, watched as they approached, and Joseph assumed it was because they were negro, blacks were not common in the territories. Joseph and Lizzie didn't hesitate as they moved toward the open gate. As they entered, two buckskin clad, whiskery faced trapper types gawked at them. Joseph saw a small sign swinging from the overhanging roof that read "Trader" and reined the mule to the hitch-rail. He whispered to Lizzie, "Git down and come with me." She slipped from her mule and tethered it, ducked under the rail and followed her brother. As they stepped to the boardwalk, Joseph stopped suddenly.

"Wal, lookee here. Whatchu doin' here, boy?" The question came from a black man with a parcel under his arm and standing spread legged in front of the trader's door. "Why, yore da fust black folks we seen outchere." He leaned to the side to look past Joseph and Lizzie and asked, "Where's yore folks, boy?"

"Uh, they back wid the wagon yonder. Pap sent us'ns in for supplies."

The big man held out his hand and said, "Well, welcome to da West! I be Dick Green. Me'n muh missus work fer the Bent's here at dare fot, and up till now, we been da' only black folks outchere."

Joseph extended his hand to shake and said, "Pleased to meetchu, Mr. Green. I'm Joseph Thomas and dis muh sister, Elizabeth Thomas."

"Well, you go 'head on and git yo' supplies. But 'fo you leave, you come see us o'er yonder," and motioned to the quarters of William Bent, "cuz my wife'll shore wanna talk to you'ns."

"Yessir, we be glad to. Good to meetchu Mr. Green," replied Joseph and stepped aside to allow him to pass. Joseph placed his hand on Lizzie's shoulder and steered her into the trader's room.

The darkness and the strange smells stymied both Joseph and Lizzie as they entered the crowded room. A few tables and chairs sat unoccupied near the far window filtering sunlight through fly specks, smoke stains, and dirt. The counter was piled with pelts of every variety and smell, while barrels of staples sat covered along the wall. The back wall held shelves of canned goods and trade goods. A portion of the wall held rifles, pistols and knives. Lizzie stared at the wondrous assortment, having never been inside any trading post or general store at any time in her life.

When the trader looked up to see the two young people, he snorted and asked, "Whatchu want?"

"Uh, we need some supplies," replied a hesitant Joseph.

"Alright, whatchu want?"

Joseph began to name off the many items he thought about, from flour, sugar, and cornmeal, powder, lead and flints. The trader listened and looked through squinted eyes as he asked, "You got money or you tradin' sumpin'?"

"I got money to pay. We could also use a couple saddles, you got any?"

"Nope, but you can git some at the stable yonder," he motioned with a head nod, as he began gathering the many items for Joseph.

"I'm also needin' a tow sack to put this stuff in, if'n you got one," he asked.

"Cost you," said the trader without hesitation.

Joseph nodded his understanding and continued looking at the many goods arrayed around the room. They gathered two sets of clothes for each and added them to the pile.

"You want five or ten pound o' flour?" asked the trader.

"Uh, ten. And ten of the cornmeal too, but five of sugar'll do," replied Joseph, and as an afterthought said, "Make that two ten pounders of each and ten of sugar."

The trader looked up but continued his gathering of the goods. In a short while, the goods were gathered, sacked and tallied. The trader looked at Joseph and said, "That'll be twelve an' a half dollars."

Joseph had taken the precaution of putting a few coins in his pocket so he wouldn't have to show his money pouch and now reached into that pocket and brought out three five dollar gold pieces and laid them on the counter. He lifted his eyes to the trader, awaiting his change. He noticed the trader look at him with a bit of surprise on his face and pulled the coins toward him.

The trader was wondering if this youngster knew numbers to know what kind of change he should be given. The trader looked at the young man, thought better of his impulse to cheat him, and gave the correct change. He was surprised when Joseph looked at the coin, counted it out and put it in his pocket. Joseph thanked the trader and with a sack over each shoulder, and Lizzie carrying one as well, they left the room. .

Tying the two sacks together, he laid them across the back of the mule, carried the third and he and Lizzie led the mules to the stable to see about saddles. When they walked into the large open door, they were greeted by a friendly "Halloo" from a large man with a leather apron stretched over a very hairy chest and under a long set of chin whiskers. A dirty skull cap fought to keep hair from his eyes, somewhat unsuccessfully, and large fists held a piece of metal on the anvil while he repeatedly dropped a hammer to shape his work. For a few moments, the Thomas' watched the blacksmith and waited until he was able to talk with them.

He set the hammer down, wiped his sweaty brow, and looked up at the two visitors as he chugged a big swig of water from a pouch. "So, what can I do ye fer?"

"Well, we need some saddles for our mules. We lost our wagon back down the trail a ways and now we need to be ridin' and saddles'd sure be a help."

The big man scowled as he looked at the two and said, "You don't know much 'bout saddles, do ya," asked the man.

"Not a lot, but we still need some," explained Joseph.

"Wal, ya see, younker, a saddle fer a mule's different from one fer a horse. See that thar wither on that mule? See, it's skinnier and taller than a horse an a reg'lar saddle ain't ver' com'fable fer 'em. Now, the way I sees it, we can do one of two things. I can sell you a couple horses an' saddles, or trade 'em fer yore mules thar. Or, I can sell you a couple mule saddles I just happen to have."

"Lemme look at them mule saddles," asked Joseph.

"They ain't much to look at, but yore mules'll like 'em," explained the smithy as he walked to the back-corner tack room. He came out holding two very dusty saddles with the leather dark, dry and cracking. As he looked down on them, he said, "Tell ya what I'll do. I'll soften' 'em up with some saddle soap, throw in the cruppers, collars and breeching, and trade you for the harness you have on 'em now and say, five dollars. How's that sound?"

Joseph reached out his hand to shake on the deal as he said, "That'll be fine. How long'll it take?"

The smithy looked at the gear, moved it about to see better, and looked up at Joseph and said, "Gimme an hour."

Joseph smiled and nodded, looked at Lizzie and motioned for her to come along as he said to the smithy, "We be back in an hour, and thank ya' suh. ."

CHARLOTTE GREEN HAD ANTICIPATED their visit and had finished her work in the kitchen. She was seated at the table when they knocked on the kitchen door. She jumped up, opened the door and looked at her visitors with a broad smile as she said, "Come in, come in. Yo sure a sight fer sore eyes. Now, sit down an' tell me all 'bout it."

Joseph looked at the enthusiastic woman and asked, "Tell you 'bout what?"

"Anything, ever'thing, thas what!" proclaimed the excited woman. "Glory be, I ain't never thot I'd see 'nother colored person ever outchere in this wild place. What brung you'ns outchere?"

As they seated themselves and Charlotte prepared a cup of cider for her guests, Joseph explained, "Well, we, our family that is, were headed to Californy but the flood took our folks an' wagon an all, so me'n Lizzie figgered we best just keep on'a goin'."

"Oh my, mercy me, you lost yo folks, thas terr'ble. But how you two young'uns gonna make it all the way to Californy? Thas a long ways!"

"Yes'm, reckon so. But we cain't go back. See, massa Thomas wuz gonna give us our manumission papers, but he gots killed fust. So, Pap said the onliest way we could stay t'gether as a fam'ly was to go to the territories or Californy. So, we just up an' left."

Charlotte looked to her husband and back at the two visitors. "So, you be runaways?"

"Reckon so, but Pap said slavery was outlawed out'chere in the territories, ain't it?"

"Well, yeah, but they's been slave catchers that tries to take any colored folks and take 'em back to make 'em slaves, even if they be free. So, you watch out, cuz ya' never know who's a catcher and who's gonna be tellin' on you," explained Charlotte.

Joseph hung his head and said, "All Pap wanted was for us to be free. He said we could find freedom on the frontier."

Dick Green interjected, "If'n you go to the mountains, mebbe make you a home up thar, mebbe the slave catchers won't git you. But, if'n you be determined to go to Californy, then you should take that trail through the mountains, yonder."

"There's a trail? Can you point us to it?" asked Joseph, hopefully.

"Yup, sure can. But, winter's comin' on and it can be bad in the mountains," he explained.

"Don't see's how we got much choice. I be thankin' you if'n you can point us in the right direction," said Joseph, hopefully. The nodding heads of Dick Green and his wife Charlotte gave him his answer.

CHAPTER TEN
CONFRONTATION

THE DAYS PASSED SWIFTLY BY, BUT THEIR HARD WORK HAD SHOWN positive results. The roof with the lodgepole pine poles for rafters and the top covering of fresh cut sod was complete and the cabin was finished to his original plan. With a fireplace of flat granite slide rock against the side wall and the chimney blending in with the overhang, Tatum thought the smoke would be easily dispersed. With the overhang directing the smoke to the tall ponderosa that shadowed the cliff face, any smoke would not be seen. Now all that remained was the building of furniture: a bed, table, chairs, shelving and a workbench near the fireplace for food preparation. There was still a good supply of the lodgepole that he would use for crafting any other needed items. But as he looked at the sky and the clouds in the distance, he thought he should start supplying up for winter. There were three main needs; meat, firewood, and fodder for the animals.

White Feather had kept herself busy working with the hides from the buffalo and even with the splint, she moved about as if unhindered. Tatum looked at her then said, "I think I'm going on a hunt for some elk. Wanna come?"

It was early, with the first light of dawn stretching over the mountain behind them. The dim glow was pushing the shadow of the cliff face beyond the trees and holding tight to the chill of the night. She looked up grinning as she explained, "These hides need working and it will take all my time and strength. You go, and I will do this." He nodded and started for the corral to ready the horses. He turned back to her,"I'm goin' down towards the pass, there's a big herd that feeds around there and I think I could get what I need. But, I might be gone overnight."

"I understand," she answered.

As he rigged the horses and secured his gear, and chuckled to himself thinking how the two of them were sounding like an old married couple. The interchange had reminded him of his Ma and Pa. He glanced back over his shoulder at White Feather and thought, *She sure is a good lookin' woman.* But he reminded himself their arrangement was just one of convenience, only until her leg healed enough for her to travel back to her people. He shrugged his shoulders as he slid the Hawken into the scabbard under the stirrup leathers, checked the bow and quiver tied on the big bay with the panniers and the pack that hung over the poles of the travois.

He swung aboard the sorrel, reined him around, and grabbing the lead rope of the bay, said, "I'm off. I hope to be back this evenin' but it might be tomorrow."

"Good hunting!"

He knew the trail to the pass would take most of the day, but he hoped to reach his spot by late afternoon, giving him ample time for a hunt in the pre-dusk hours when the elk would come from the timber to graze in the valley below. The big animals would often snooze during the warm time of the day, then feed and go to water in the early and late hours. Every time he rode through the pass, he'd see several elk and hope there would be many still browsing in the area.

The creak of leather and the rolling gait of the sorrel gave Tatum a certain comfort. The occasional click of hooves against rocks, intermittent snorts from the horses, the cool breeze of fall brushing his face and the incredible views of the mountains with their fall skirts of golden aspen brought a smile to his face. He was happy, happy with his life and his choice for a home, happy with friends he made and plans fulfilled. He believed if his Pa and Ma could see him now, they would be mighty proud, and happy for him. The sudden stop of his sorrel jolted him from his reverie. The uplifted head with ears forward of his mount told of the animal's alarm The scattering of juniper gave little cover to a black shadow that rambled up the slight slope toward the mountain. A big sow black bear swung her head side to side and ambled along with her pigeon-toed walk. Tatum thought about taking the bear, but knew if he did he would forfeit the hunt for the elk. He chose meat over fat, but thought he would have to make a hunt for a bear to get the needed fat for grease and even the meat to add to his larder. The horses watched, but more out of curiosity than fear, and the bear soon disappeared into the thicker trees. Tatum gigged his mount forward and they continued on the trail.

JOSEPH AND LIZZIE were pleased with themselves, what with the new supplies, saddles and renewed hopes for their journey. The saddles made their travel much more endurable and the attitude of the mules showed they seemed to appreciate the gear more. It took Joseph a couple of tries before he got the rigging down, having to put the crupper under their tails, the breeching behind their rumps and the breast collar across their chest, it was more than he was used to, but once done, he was pleased with his work.

They had resumed their practice of traveling at night and resting during the day and now almost a week since their stop at Bent's fort, they were making their camp in the pines of the mountains. After Dick Green pointed out the cut in the stone that harbored the pass into the San Luis valley, the distant range had loomed as their dusk and dawn landmarks. But now they had entered the rocky terrain and the cool air of the night and the sweet smell of pine made this first camp in the Rockies a memorable one.

They had rested well, wrapped in the new blankets from the fort, and now Joseph sat on a log at the edge of the fire waiting for the coffee to be ready. Dusk was approaching, and they would soon make ready for another night's travel. From the vantage point on the slight shoulder with the clear view of the valley below, Joseph thought this night's travel would be easy as they crossed the broad expanse of the San Luis valley. He was quickly learning that the thin air made the judging of distances difficult, as it seemed when they left the fort and traveled toward the mountains, it would be no more than a day or two before they reached the distant landmark. But it took almost a week, slowly drawing nearer with each day's travel. Now, looking at the valley below, he thought better of underestimating the distance across the flats.

Lizzie stirred just as Joseph put the frying pan with the leftover cornpone near the fire. She stretched and yawned, dropped the blanket and made her way into the trees to tend to her business. When she returned she looked around and said, "These mountains sure are big, ain't they?"

"Yup, they is. Ain't never thought about 'em 'afore, but they's purty too."

"Mr. Green said it might be a good thing to just hole up in these here mountains, what with winter comin' on," said Lizzie, looking at her brother from the corner of her eye.

"If'n we was, where'd we stay? Ain't got no cabin or nuthin', and cain't sleep out in the open. Mr. Green says the snow gets deep up hyar."

"I dunno, I'se just sayin's all," answered Lizzie.

They both sat and stared into the flames, letting their minds drift and questions ramble through their thoughts. The mesmerizing dance of the fire was interrupted by the gurgle of the coffee pot announcing its work had begun. Joseph reached over to move the pot back a little from the flames, adjusted the frying pan, and put his elbows on his knees to support his chin with his palms to resume his fire-stare. They wouldn't start their travel until dusk had loosed its grip on the daylight, and the remaining hours of light would be ample for them to finish their meal and pack their gear.

———

TATUM LOOKED at the lowering sun and believed his timing was just right. Tethering his horses in a small clearing just inside the tree line, he prepared himself for the hunt. He used the sling on the Hawken to swing the rifle to his back, put the Paterson in its holster at his waist, hung the quiver of arrows at his side, and stepped into his longbow to bend the limbs and place the string in the nocks. Satisfied with his preparations, he moved silently into the trees, staying close to the edge of the tree-line to maintain a view of the wide clearing. Grass was abundant in the mountains meadow and the gurgling stream cascaded down the rocky bed, inviting thirsty animals to partake. Tatum found a well-protected spot that gave a clear view and space for shooting and settled himself to wait for the elk.

The sun was cradled in the distant mountains and the thin clouds captured the colors and spread the orange and gold across the horizon reaching to the canopy of fading blue when the first tentative steps of a cow elk brought her into the grassy valley. She was the matriarch, and as she moved to the headwaters of the Sangre de Cristo creek for her evening drink, she was followed by the rest of the small herd. Tatum counted twelve mature cows trailed by yearling calves, several of last year's calf crop with the young bulls sporting their spike antlers, and a couple of young cows that were herded by the big bull as he waggled his massive antlers through the aspen.

Tatum waited until the animals were comfortable with their grazing and drinking before he chose his targets. A young bull with spikes of about sixteen inches would be his first target and one of the two young cows would be the other. As the rest of the herd neared the creek, it brought them within less than fifty yards of Tatum's promontory. He slowly moved away from the trunk of the gnarly fir shield, laid his body into the longbow and let fly the deadly missile. As the arrow whispered its way to its mark, Tatum was already nocking the next. The first found its target in the neck of the young bull, and the animal lifted itself from its spread-legged stance at the edge of the water and whirled around to take flight. The sudden movement alerted the rest of the herd, but that moment's hesitation brought the young cow into Tatum's sight and an arrow was sent on its way.

Tatum saw it find its target just behind the front leg.the shaft sunk deep into the chest of the cow as she too whirled about to t. Tatum nocked another arrow as he watched the herd scamper to the trees, and saw the young bull stagger and stumble, regain his footing and walk two more steps before falling chin down and crumpling into a pile. The young cow ran with the fletching of the arrow flashing at her side, the arrow looking like a bird of prey had sunk its talons into its fur. Tatum followed the cow with the second arrow drawn to its full length, and when the cow hesitated a step, he sent the arrow to find purchase and split the ribs of the cow. The impact made the cow stumble, stagger and fall. Tatum had already nocked another arrow, but saw no necessity as he stepped from the tree and walked, holding the leather wrapped grip and the arrow with one hand. He heard the cracking and rattling of the timber as the herd thrashed through the aspen and pine to make their getaway.

Suddenly he heard a scream and another, followed by a shout and additional crashing of timber. Tatum stopped and stared at the timber, surprised to hear the scream of a human, knowing the only time an Indian would scream would be during a charge into battle, but this was more of a scream from a girl in fright and the shout was from another. With a glance, he saw the two elk were down and dead, but he started into a trot toward the trees, holding his bow across his chest with the right hand holding the arrow at the nock, ready to use the weapon if necessary.

CHAPTER ELEVEN
RESCUE

Startled by the crashing of the timber as the elk herd charged uphill through the pines, Joseph stood looking in wonder at what was making the noise. Lizzie jumped to his side as they watched through the trees. Suddenly the herd, led by the matriarch cow, crashed through the trees and directly towards the shocked siblings. Lizzie screamed but before the two could move , the herd stampeded through the clearing and knocked the pair to the ground. Sharp hooves struck them again and again as the panicked animals stumbled blindly on following their lead cow. Hurting and fearful, the two siblings looked to one another, but as they struggled to lift themselves from the ground amidst the scattered coals and ashes of the fire, the big herd bull, grunting and kicking, charged the larger target before him.

The massive wapiti lowered his antlers and with crazed eyes and tongue lolling to the side, he dug his hooves as he sought to impale the offender with his sharp antlers. With seven sharp points on each side, antlers were deadly. Joseph flung himself to the side, yet the bull pierced him with one tine through the shoulder. The bull lifted his head with Joseph on the antlers and flung the burden to the side of the clearing. He lowered his head again, eyes on the smaller target, dug his hooves into the ground, throwing dirt over his rump and charged. But Lizzie was quicker and dropped prone alongside and behind the log that had been used for a bench beside the fire. The big bull hit the log, moved it a few inches, lifted his head and swung it back and forth. He snorted his disgust and trotted from the clearing in triumph. Lizzie watched the yellow rump disappear into the trees and pushed herself up. She examined herself, seeing the tears in her gingham and feeling the bruised chest and arms.Struggling to take a breath she looked for her brother. There, near the big tree, lay Joseph, face in the dirt and blood spreading over his back. Lizzie struggled to her feet and stumbled to her brother's side, reassured to see he was breathing. She reached for his shoulder and dropping to her knees, she struggled to pull Joseph to his back. A moan escaped his lips as she rolled him over, his eyes fluttered but he didn't speak.

"Joseph, Joseph, wake up Joseph," cried Lizzie, terrified at the injuries and wonderingwhat she could do, all alone in the wilderness.

His ragged breath came in snatches and another moan slipped from his lips. Lizzie looked at her brother, tried to shake him to consciousness, but failing to revive him, she dropped her head in sobs. She was so scared and felt so helpless, and she hurt. She looked at her lap and saw blood seeping through the cloth by her thigh; her leg had been skinned, scraped and peeled, revealing raw and bleeding flesh. It was an effort to move but she tried to find a more comfortable position so she could breathe better, and she felt something at her cheek, put her hand to her face and brought it away bloody.

A voice startled her, and she lifted her head to see a man walking towards her. He spoke, "You're hurt. Let me help you." Her wide eyes fluttered, and she fell back against her brother, and darkness closed over her.

TATUM WORKED QUICKLY, using what was available to bandage the two injured siblings. He moved the brother to a prone position, washed his wound and packed it with a quickly made poultice of sage leaves and buffalo grass. He washed the other lesser wounds, made the young man as comfortable as possible and turned to the girl. Washing her wounds, he could tell she had some broken ribs, but nothing more serious that he could tell. With the initial care done, he started a small fire and left to tend to the downed elk.

He had never worked so fast before, but he quickly dressed the elk, deboning the carcasses and bundling the meat into the hides and securing them to the travois. Once done, he rode back to the clearing and the two injured people. The girl sat up and watched him approach. He dropped to the ground at her side, introducing himself, "I'm Tate. I'm going to take you to my cabin, so we can tend to you and your friend here."

"He's my brother. I'm Lizzie and he's Joseph," she said, shyly looking at their rescuer.

"Did you have horses?" asked Tatum.

"Mules, day was back that-a-way," she motioned toward a break in the trees. "We had 'em tied, but don't know now."

The saddles lay at the edge of the clearing and the two mules looked at the newcomer with curiosity and heightened ears. Tatum looked at them, back at the saddles and began to speak to the animals. Within a short while, the mules were saddled and geared up and Tatum led them back to the clearing.

It was a struggle, but Tatum and Lizzie finally had Joseph secured to his saddle aboard a mule and tied down with strips of blanket so he could make the trip to the cabin. Lizzie climbed aboard and was able to sit her saddle, as she bravely forced herself to hold on tight. Any sudden movement brought a moan, but she was determined to make the ride.

They were used to traveling at night and the big moon gave a welcome relief to the journey. The quietness was broken by the questions of the great horned owl, a pair of coyotes sassed one another, and the caterwaul of mountain lion caught the attention of the horses and mules. It was a peaceful night, but a trying night for both Lizzie and the unconscious Joseph.

The rising sun had yet to make itself known when the caravan of travelers made its way into the clearing of the cabin. White Feather stepped from beside the cabin, bow and nocked arrow at the ready, but recognized Tatum and dropped the weapon as she walked quickly to the side of his sorrel and lifted her face in question. He smiled down at her and began to explain, "I shot a couple elk, but the herd stampeded right over the top of the camp of these two and they're hurt pretty bad. They need some tendin' to, and I thought you might like some extra work."

She grinned at his description, and as Tatum swung his leg over the rump of the sorrel, she made her way to the injured Joseph. Lizzie was struggling to get down and Tatum reached up to help the girl. White Feather had undone the strips of blanket that held Joseph to the saddle and Tatum reached her side as Joseph slid from the saddle.

As they worked to make the pair comfortable on bedrolls under the ponderosa, the big pine needles providing a comfortable base, Tatum explained the injuries to White Feather. He knew the woman was an experienced healer and would readily know the needed plants for ministering to the pair. She went right to work, changing the bandage and poultice on Joseph, cleaning the other wounds and making note of the needs. She worked by the firelight that had been used for their cookfire and had been rekindled by Tatum. When she turned to Lizzie, the girl was already fast asleep on the bedroll and White Feather covered her over, knowing rest would be the best medicine for now.

With both patients sleeping, Tatum and White Feather sat across from one another with the campfire between them. She had put on a pot of coffee and listened attentively as Tatum explained in more detail about the hunt and the rescue of the duo. She looked at her friend and said, "You should be a medicine man, a shaman."

"What? Why do you say that? I don't have no hankerin' for that."

She shook her head and grinned at the thought and added, "Wherever you go, you find people that are hurt or ill or in need and you always help them."

"Well, ain't that what you're s'posed to do? Help people?"

"Not everybody would do that," explained Feather, smiling at her benevolent friend.

Tatum looked at the sky that showed the beginning grey of morning and attempted to change the subject of their conversation, "It's gettin' light. We need to find them plants an' such that you need fer them," nodding his head in the direction of the two.

"You can get them. I will tell you what is needed, but you can get them," and she looked to the girl as she said, "the little one will need her ribs bound up tight. She has broken at least two of them that I can tell, maybe more. She is lucky she was not killed when the elk ran over her." She looked at Tatum, expecting some response and received only a nod of his head. "The hole in his shoulder," she motioned to Joseph, "will take a lot of poultices and maybe I will need to sew it together. I believe he also has some broken ribs. It will take some time for them to heal."

"Yeah, I'm sure it will. And that'll make sleepin' arrangements difficult."

"I thought about that. We should make a wickiup next to the cabin for more room. You and the man will sleep in the wickiup and the girl will sleep with me in the cabin."

Tatum looked at her with a scowl wrinkling his forehead and said, "You mean to tell me I went to all the work of building a cabin and I ain't even going to be able to use it?"

She grinned at his remark and said, "I have never seen people of this color before. Is it common where you come from?"

Tatum had never thought about the seclusion of the Comanche people, especially the women, and was somewhat surprised that she had never seen a negro. He started to explain, "Yes, it is common. But most of them are made slaves, similar to what your people do with captives. I guess you could say it's like they are from a different tribe. Just like your people are different from the Apache and the Kiowa."

White Feather looked toward the prone figure of Joseph and said, "His hair reminds me of the buffalo."

Tatum looked in the direction of the pair and nodding his head, replied, "Yeah, I guess so. Never thought much about it though, but I reckon you're right."

The coffee was ready and the two friends each had a cup of the black java, enjoying the quiet of the morning together. In a short while, White Feather struggled to her feet with the aid of the crutch, handed the water bag and the canteen to Tatum and gave him instructions to his plant gathering and sent him on his way.

"Oh, and please to cut several of those willows for drying racks for the elk," she instructed as he walked away from the camp, taking the trail down to the creek. She knew this would be a busy day with tending to the patients and preparing the meat of the elk.

CHAPTER TWELVE
INJURED

White Feather pulled the hide of the elk over the edge of the upright slide rock. She had propped it between two other flat stones and was using the long straight edge to stretch the elk hides she treated with the brain slurry. Lizzie watched from the log near the fire pit and asked, "what does that do?"

White Feather looked at the curious girl that was quickly becoming a friend. For three days Lizzie and her brother Joseph had been tended to by both White Feather and Tatum. The girl, with her rib cage still wrapped tight, was healing well. Joseph was taking a little longer with the wound from the elk antler in his shoulder. White Feather had opted to sew the large wound and pack it in healing poultices made of the inner bark of the ponderosa and a few other ingredients garnered from her years of experience. His ribs were also bound and while Joseph napped on his bedroll, the women were busy with the hides, one working and the other watching and learning. Tatum left early that morning for another hunt and was expected back by dusk.

"This stretches the hide and makes it soft. It also cleans the tanning mixture from the inside."

"That one ain't got no hair like the buffalo, why?" asked the girl.

"The buffalo makes a warm robe or blanket; the elk hides make better moccasins and other things. It is not as thick as the buffalo and we can work it easier."

"Is that all you gots to do?"

"No, after this, we will smoke it. It will make it even softer and helps when it gets wet," explained White Feather, pleased with Lizzie's curiosity.

"Mebbe after these ribs get better, I can hep ya," suggested the girl.

"Well, after I am finished with this hide, we will look for the plants for food and healing," declared White Feather, recalling Lizzie's inquiries about the poultices. The girl smiled at White Feather and drew closer to watch the woman work.

TATUM LAY motionless in the willow thicket, watching the hunting party of Jicarilla Apache. He counted twelve hunters, leading five packhorses loaded with carcasses of deer and elk. Tatum saw the scouts before the rest of the party and was quick to take cover in the willows. His horses were tethered well back in the trees and could not be seen. Tatum had taken two deer and after seeing sign of buffalo, had walked to the stream side to see if there was any additional sign that would indicate a more recent passing of the wooly brutes. It was then he saw the scouts making their way around the beaver ponds. As the party passed, he heard them talking in low tones, apparently sharing stories and laughing at one another, trusting in the scouts to alert them of any game.

Tatum was surprised to see Apache this far north in the valley. White Feather had explained the Apache and Comanche were usually not enemies, often allied together for a common purpose, but the Jicarilla territory was the far southern and western part of the valley and the Apache usually hunted west of the Rio Grande in the southern San Juan mountains. Having had no friendly contact with the Apache, Tatum wasn't taking any chances and stayed well hidden in the thick willows.

He watched through the overhanging branches as the hunting party continued north along the creek bed, moving in and out as the beaver ponds demanded. When well out of sight, Tatum slowly moved from his cover, always watching in the direction of the Apache, and stealthily made his way back to his horses. Although he wanted more game, he chose to start his return to his cabin, staying well in the deep timber along the hips of the Sangre de Cristo mountains. Carefully picking the lesser used game trails, he chose a route that would be difficult to follow and often stepped down to cover his sign. He knew any tracker worth his salt could easily follow his trail, but since no one was particularly following, he wanted to obscure as much sign of his passing as possible.

He looked over his right shoulder to see the sun slipping from behind the wispy clouds and dropping towards the distant horizon. He calculated he was still over an hour from camp and knew he had ample daylight left. The trail broke into the open, facing a boulder strewn shoulder with scattered fir and aspen, and he pushed the sorrel into the clearing. He looked at the trail, decided to try again to obscure any sign of his passing and stepped down from the saddle. The Hawken rested in the scabbard and he carried the longbow across his pommel and out of habit, kept it in his hand as he walked back toward the bay.

Suddenly a shadow passed over him and he looked to see a mountain lion land on the hips of the bay, sinking his long claws into the meaty rump of the travois laden horse. The horse reared up, screamed and kicked, hitting only the travois, but launched himself after the spooked sorrel. Tatum frantically grabbed at an arrow and hurriedly nocked it, drawing the bow for a shot all in one motion. The arrow sailed over the lion, but the horse bucking and kicking and the travois bouncing around, the cat lost its grip and dropped to the ground beside the trail, spinning around to face the man. Tatum snatched another arrow and slapped it beside the hand grip as he looked to the string to nock it. As he started to raise the bow, the cat was upon him and all he saw were teeth. The cougar wrapped legs and claws around

Tatum's shoulders, bearing him to the ground. The arrow had dug itself into the neck of the cat but not far enough to stay the attack and snapped in two with the weight of the cougar. Tatum knew a lion's tactic was to bring its hind feet to rip the guts from it prey, but Tatum twisted to the side as he grabbed at the Bowie in the sheath at his back. The teeth of the cat dug into his neck and shoulder, but the adrenaline-fueled man was fighting for his life and plunged the razor-sharp blade of the bowie between the ribs of his attacker. Again and again he plunged the knife while forcing his fingers into the side of the mouth of the cougar, trying to pry his teeth from his shoulder. Claws from the rear leg of the cat caught in the belt and holster with the Paterson and ripped it to the ground. Tatum brought the Bowie to the Cougar's throat, thrust it in and drew it back, cutting the neck muscles and almost decapitating the cat, causing it to release its grip and roll to the side of Tatum.

An exhausted Tatum lay back, trying to get his breath and slowly began to take stock of his wounds. Blood was streaming down his shoulder and arm, he felt the deep punctures and tears at his back and at his hip. The worst was his neck and shoulder. He rolled to his hands and knees, struggled to replace the knife in the scabbard, and staggered to his feet. He bent to pick up his bow, fell face first into a clump of grass and everything went black.

WHEN THE HORSES, obviously spooked, trotted into the clearing of the cabin, tossing their heads and prancing nervously. White Feather jumped to her feet in alarm. She quickly looked from one to the other, caught the trailing reins of the sorrel and spoke softly as she patted his neck to settle him down. Lizzie had awkwardly stood and stumbled to the bay and mimicked White Feather as she caught the lead rope of the pack horse. White Feather looked the sorrel over, saw no injuries or blood that would indicate Tatum was injured, then looked to the bay. She instantly spotted the deep gouges from the lion's claws and knew what happened. The cougar had probably smelled the fresh meat, stalked and attacked. Tatum was either afoot or injured and she needed to go to him. But first she had to take care of the bay. She sent Lizzie for the poultices and bandages while she tied off the sorrel to the corral fence, took the bay from Lizzie and quickly dropped the travois, led the bay into the corral and tied him fast to the pole fence. She swiftly applied the herbal salve and covered the wound with a muddy pack that would cool the animal and begin the healing. Satisfied with the temporary fix, she swung aboard the sorrel and told Lizzie, "I must go to Tatum," and dug her heels into the ribs of the sorrel.

CHAPTER THIRTEEN
DISCOVERY

Fear filled White Feather'sheart as she dug heels into the ribs of the big sorrel. Her only thought was Tatum. With the deep claw marks on the rump of the bay, she knew there had been an attack by a mountain lion, and with Tatum missing, anything could have happened. She looked over her left shoulder to see the fading light along the western horizon and her dread mounted. Without slowing, she leaned along the neck of the sorrel, eyeing the trail to assure herself they were still following the back trail of the fleeing horses. Hooves clattered on the rocky trail, limbs of fir and ponderosa seemed to reach out and try to pluck her from the saddle. She broke into a glade with scattered aspen, allowing her to see farther on the trail but there was no sign.

The sorrel was slowing his pace, and White Feather thought he was tiring, but his uplifted head, taut neck and ears forward warned her. She slowed him to a fast walk, but he stutter-stepped aas they broke into the slide rock slope. White Feather reined up and slipped to the ground, taking her bow in hand and nocking an arrow. She knelt, and ground tied the sorrel, placing a stone on the reins for added assurance. In a crouch, she moved forward along the trail, searching the tall boulders and trees at the side of the slope for any movement.

She moved soundlessly and in the shadow of the boulder, she saw a familiar unmoving form. With a quick search of her surroundings, she kicked her mount to run to the side of the prone figure of Tatum. She slid to the ground to examine the man. Blood was everywhere, she scanned his wounds, rolled him to his back and a moan and fluttering eyes said he was alive. His chest was free, but his back was torn and gouged, as were his shoulder and neck. There was blood in his hair and down his cheek, his left hand was covered with dried blood and his hip and leg had the buckskin britches torn away and the long gouges showed patches of blood.

With light fading quickly, White Feather stripped the britches from Tatum, cut them into wide strips and bound up his hip and leg, rolled his tunic up to cover the wounds of his back and wrapped them tight with a strip of buckskin from his britches. He was semi-conscious as White Feather said, "I must get you up on your horse to get back to the cabin soon. Can you help?"

"Uhhh . . . yeah, maybe, let's try."

They struggled together, both ending up bloody and exhausted, but they were soon on their way back to the camp, White Feather riding behind Tatum and holding him in the saddle. Lizzie had banked the fire and sat on the log staring into the flames. The girl jumped to her feet and ran to the side of the sorrel, reaching up to touch Tatum and recoiling at the sight of his bloodied body. She looked to White Feather and the woman said, "Take the reins of the sorrel, and then you can help me with Tatum." Feather slipped to the ground and caught Tatum as he started to topple. Joseph had roused and come to the side of Feather, trying to help but his weakness was more of a hindrance.

Tatum was soon settled on a bedroll near the fire and White Feather started her ministrations, cleaning the wounds, applying poultices and bandaging the worst. She winced as Tatum moaned and flinched. The gouges from the claws were deep, but she chose to apply poultices and bind them tightly and would wait till daylight for a decision about stitching. She was more concerned about the bite marks on the shoulder and neck, knowing the chances for infection was greatest with those wounds. She finished her work, brewed Tatum some tea from amaranth leaves, and set back to watch her patient struggle with finding some comfort. He sipped his tea, looked to White Feather and said, "Thanks for comin' to get me. You might wanna go back an' get that hide in the mornin'."

White Feather nodded, "You sleep, I will get more plants for you in the light."

He lay back and pulled the blanket up over his shoulder and was soon asleep. White Feather sat quiet and watched the sleeping figure before her, questioning her attachment to this man. He had been a friend that helped her people, and she was his teacher of the Shoshonean language of her people, the Comanche. When she broke her leg during the buffalo hunt, Tatum kept her at his camp and tended her while she mended, she thought as she rubbed her hand along her leg, so recently freed of its splint. But was this more than a mutually beneficial friendship?

She rose and fetched her bedroll to stretch it out near Tatum and the fire, convincing herself it was just to be near in case she was needed in the night. She lay down, propped herself on her elbows, looked over the fire to her patient, smiled, and lay back to find sleep for the night. She stared at the starry canopy for a long time, letting her mind wander about the different paths her future might take, but slumber soon closed her eyes.

IT WAS JUST over a week since the cougar attack and Tatum was sore, but healing, and becoming very restless. White Feather and Lizzie were off on a plant hunt to replenish the many they used for the healing of just about everyone. White Feather had rid herself of the splint and crutch, but still struggled a mite, but with Lizzie always at her side, the two women managed to have successful hunts for the many needs of the two remaining patients.

The air was telling of the coming of winter by leaving a touch of frost every morning and Tatum was now not just restless, but concerned. Although he had brought in considerable meat that had been smoked and dried by White Feather, there was still the matter of safely storing it for the winter months. His original plan was to build racks and shelving in the mouth of the cavern, but his injuries had waylaid that. He thought about them now and believed this would be a good time for a more thorough exploration of the cave, accessed through the cleft behind the cabin.

He had been cautioned by White Feather to limit his movement as not to open the wounds. It had taken several days of washing and letting the wounds bleed freely to rid them of any possible contamination from the cougar's teeth and claws, but they were healing nicely now. White Feather had retrieved the carcass for the pelt and saw the lion was an old and injured one with several broken teeth and claws as well as missing the toes on his left rear foot, which kept him from disemboweling Tatum. The young man of the mountains was sore but his frustration at his inactivity drove him on.

He broke off two sap laden branches from a ponderosa at the edge of the clearing, fashioning them into torches. When he completed the torches, he entered the cleft in the cliff face that would take him into the cave. With one torch lit, he pushed into the cavernous maw of darkness, taking slow tentative steps. Having already fashioned some racks and placed them just inside the cave, he saw White Feather had placed the large cuts of the the buffalo and elk well off the ground on the higher reaches of the racks. He smiled at the thought of the woman and all she had done during his recovery. But he also noted more racks would be needed for a good winter's supply of meat.

As he passed the racks, the tunnel like entrance began to widen into the cavern he had briefly explored. He often had to step across and through a trickle of spring water that flowed from the depths but pushing on he was surprised at the size of the cavern. He paused and lifted the torch for a better look, marveling at the stalactites and stalagmites. With the rumply pattern of the stalagmites, he was reminded of the wide dresses seen on fashionable ladies in the cities. The hanging stalactites seemed to threaten anything below with impalement as tiny rivulets of water dripped from the slender tips. It was easy to imagine the formations as strange creatures of the deep. The shadows cast by the torch gave the cavern a mysterious appearance. The colors ranged from a dull tan to deep reds and Tatum thought they had been painted by the creator just to amaze anyone that was fortunate enough to lay their eyes on them.

The far end of the large cavern revealed two tunnel-like openings deeper into the mountain. One was the keeper of the water that flowed from the cave and the other appeared to follow the direction of the ridge of mountains overhead. He continued to follow the stream deeper into the cavern and the offshoot tunnel. It was the larger of the two, measuring about twenty feet wide and fifteen feet high at its peak. The many stalagmites and stalactites gave the appearance of a stony forest, casting shadows that moved with the light of the torch. The tracks in the sand were many, but the large tracks of a massive grizzly were the most recent. The droppings of rodents, raccoons, marmots, rats and mice, littered the floor and the occasional piles of bear scat made Tatum careful with his steps.

He entered another cavern and paused for a thorough survey. Similar in appearance but smaller than the main cavern, this harbored several beds of hibernating animals, mostly of bears. Although bears of the same species would sometimes share hibernating quarters, seldom would grizzly share with black bear or any other of the numerous smaller creatures. Tatum walked to the far wall to the bed of a grizzly with piles of scat well off to the side, but hair and claw marks in profusion. Several bones were scattered about, obviously from previous feasts by the many cave dwellers but a couple caught the eye of Tatum. He picked up what was apparently a leg bone from a human, examined it and while holding it, searched the rest of the cavern for others. Seeing white near a back wall, not too far from the wall that bled the water from the spring, he walked closer. Partially buried in a pile of small sticks, tufts of fur, and other loose items, was the skull of a man, blank eye sockets staring at the ceiling.

Tatum used the leg bone to move things aside and scratch in the dirt for any evidence of the identity of the man. As he dug, he unearthed two additional skulls and many other bones as well as scraps of leather, a long piece of metal, a portion of a leather pouch, and more bones. He sat back on his heels, trying to examine his finds in the fading light of the torch, now stuck in the sand and burning down. He fingered the pieces of leather and the strip of metal, curious about the ones that carried them into the cavern. He put them in a pouch, lit his second torch and started back. There was still the second tunnel to explore.

Tatum turned into the dry tunnel. The shaft was taller than he could reach, wide enough to ride two horses side-by-side, and the floor was sandy but without any tracks of rodents or any other creature, only slight indentations indicated tracks from long ago. Which puzzled Tatum, as the entire entry way and cavern and other tunnel held an abundance of animal tracks. Within less than twenty yards, Tatum was brought to a sudden stop. Looming before him and completely blocking the tunnel, was a large wooden plank door with hammered steel hardware. The door was seven feet by four feet and hung by three rusty steel hinges and held fast by a similar hasp and ancient padlock. As Tatum drew near, he looked the door and frame over, seeing the handiwork of ancient craftsmen. The entire tunnel was sealed by this barrier and as Tatum pushed and tugged against the blockade, he wondered how it came to be and what it was hiding. He saw the marks of grizzly claws but nothing that would tell the secret. The strength of the door would take some doing to get through and now with his second and last torch burning down and starting to sputter, he turned to leave. As he exited the dry tunnel, he noticed what appeared as another entrance to the cavern that had caved in, maybe this was the original entry in years past.

But those explorations would have to wait until another day, his torch was fading fast. As he exited the cleft, he sucked deep of the fresh air and filled his lungs with the sweet-smelling pine-scented air and leaned against the wall of the cliff to feel the warmth of the sun baked rock face. He dropped the bits of leather and piece of steel found in the cave by the door of the cabin for later examination, and walked to the fire pit to take a seat on the log to rest a bit before the return of White Feather and Lizzie. She would no doubt want to re-examine his wounds and probably change the dressings. He smiled at the thought of her ministrations and how the time with her had been so beneficial to everyone. He reached to push the coffee pot closer to the coals, added a couple of sticks to the fire, and sat back to rest.

CHAPTER FOURTEEN
STOCKPILING

WITH ANOTHER WEEK OF HEALING, BOTH JOSEPH AND TATUM WERE readying themselves for another hunt before winter set in with a fury. The tops of the Sangre's and the distant San Juan's had already been dusted with winter's warning. They now showed white against the cobalt blue of the morning sky as a notice to the small group of recovering mountaineers. The last week had been spent building a brush hut wickiup beside the cabin as sleeping quarters for the men. Supervised by White Feather, the structure was solidly built to withstand the forces of winter, although not as sturdy as the cabin where they would spend most of the winter hours.

Tatum and Joseph had the horses saddled and the mules geared up to pack as they said their goodbyes to White Feather and Lizzie, who were to spend the day gathering more roots and plants as well as rabbits and maybe some beaver to add to the larder. White Feather wanted to have more rabbit and beaver fur for winterizing their clothing and teaching Lizzie more about tanning and sewing. It had gone unspoken, but it was assumed the four would be spending the entire winter together. They had become sort of a wilderness family. Tatum smiled at the thought of so many together in what he previously believed would be a one-man cabin and a winter of solitude, but he was enjoying the company.

White Feather had shared with Tatum that the upper reaches of the San Luis valley was a preferred winter graze for the elk, a place where her people had often hunted for the royalty of the woods, so called because their coat appeared as a cape and the antlers as a crown That was Tatum's chosen destination for what might be the last hunt of the fall. The aspens were shedding their gold leaves and the mountains were cloaked in the white of early winter snows; this was the time of the elk herding together for the winter. The big bulls would have gathered their harems and the cows were ready for breeding with expected births after the green-up came. With the meat already on hand, Tatum thought two more elk would make the winter's larder sufficient. And if they happened to bag a bear before they disappeared to their hibernations, all the better.

Tatum led the way from the camp, looking back over his shoulder to see the women strapping on packs for gathering the roots and other plants to supplement their winter's stores. White Feather had become like a mother to Lizzie and was enjoying teaching the young woman the ways of the wilderness. She had shared with Tatum that she thought Lizzie would make an excellent healer and that she was a quick learner. White Feather was also fashioning a bow and arrows for the girl, anticipating teaching her the use of the preferred weapon of silent hunting. Tatum grinned at the fussing of the women as they prepared for their hunt, looked to Joseph and was pleased with the recovery of the man who was quickly becoming a friend. His wounds had been severe, and his shoulder was still limited in movement, but he was a determined young man and was committed to doing his part in preparing for the winter in the mountains.

TATUM HAD EXPLAINED the route they were taking and that this hunt might take as long as a week, but Joseph was anxious to be out and about after the many days spent abed as he recovered. And a hunt for the elk would be a good experience for the greenhorn to the mountains, he chuckled as he thought of the expression, greenhorn, and the first time he heard it was from Tatum as he sat beside the fire explaining the ways of the mountains that he himself was still learning. Joseph remembered the care and treatment he received from this man and the woman, White Feather.He recalled wondering why they cared so much and were willing to go the lengths they had, just to see to the recovery of a complete stranger, or strangers, as he considered his sister as well. They had never been treated so kindly by people of different races, especially by a white man. He remembered the many times his father had tried to convince him that not all people of a certain group, race or belief, were alike and that there were good and bad people of all kinds. Now he was beginning to understand at least some of his father's teachings were finding root in Joseph's mind.

The thick growths of pine, spruce and fir that hung from the hips of the mountains of the Sangre de Cristo, appeared like a woman's skirts; flared at the bottom and draped over the contours of the low reaches. But the black timber terminated at timberline to reveal the granite tops of the mountain range that looked like a row of stone soldiers standing guard over the valley below. The ragged hem of the pine skirts showed the occasional streambed used by snowmelt in the spring, and the many ridges and ravines outstretched below the black timber. Those same ridges were decorated with scattered juniper and pinyon that competed for water with the encroaching sage, scrub oak, and rabbitbrush of the flats. And it was along the edge of the thick timber line that Tatum and Joseph followed the game trail used by so many mountain dwelling animals as they made their way from graze to graze.

Tatum led them across the valley to the entrance of a smaller one that held Kerber Creek. This had been suggested by White Feather with the thought that if there were any buffalo left, this far north that the valley of the Kerber would be the most likely place to find them. the wooly beasts yielded more meat than any other animal so this route was well worth the effort. Tatum remembered seeing fresh buffalo sign the last time he was in the valley for a hunt, but that was also when he saw the Apache hunting party. White Feather had also warned him that the mountains on this west side of the valley were the territory of several different bands of the Ute Indians. Hopefully this hunt would only yield meat and not conflict with either the Ute or the Apache.

It was twilight by the time the two hunters found a campsite in the mouth of the valley of Kerber Creek. A cluster of juniper gave cover and shelter sufficient for the men and animals. Joseph tethered out the horses , giving them ample lead to graze and drink, while Tatum prepared the fire and readied their meal. They were content with leftover biscuits and some smoked meat to go with the fresh-brewed coffee. With several large stones nearby, they found seats near the fire and enjoyed the time to learn more about one another.

"So, you and your family were on the Thomas farm, the one just north of Cape Girardeau?" asked Tatum, flabbergasted at the comment made by Joseph as he described his beginning of this trip west.

Joseph looked at Tatum, surprised that he knew of the farm and nodded apprehensively and replied, "Yassuh, dat's right. Massuh Thomas had promised my Pap dat he was gonna have the manumission papers made up fo' us, but he gots killed in a buggy wreck. So, we'un's up an' left outta dere in a hurry. If'n we'd stayed on, we'd be sold and our fam'bly split up, an Pap didn't want that happenin'. He said slavery was not 'lowed in the territories, so here we be."

Tatum looked thoughtfully at Joseph and said, "Well, me an' my pa weren't slaves, but we wanted to come outchere for the same reason. It's what Pa called, Frontier Freedom. Just the freedom for each man, no matter what he was or anything, could be whatever he made himself to be and know real freedom. My Pa was a teacher and knew a lot about people in all the other countries of the world and how freedom was what every man wanted. He said many wars had been fought for that very reason."

"We lived in Cape Girardeau, that's where my Ma died, and then we went to Springfield. That's where my Pa was killed. So, I struck out from there and come west." He looked away from the fire and pointed to the Sangre's and said, "See how the light from the sunset's shinin' on the snow up on top o' them mountains? They say, that's how they got their name. Seems a priest with the early Spaniards saw that 'bout the time the Indians were attackin' and thought it looked like blood, and he said, 'Sangre de Cristo', or blood of Christ, just before he died."

"What 'bout all them injuns? How come they's allus attackin' an' killin' folks? White Feather ain't like that," asked Joseph.

"Well, those Indians that attacked the Spaniards were risin' up against them cuz they was makin' slaves outta the injuns and makin' 'em work in mines an such, lookin' fer gold. But the Indians got tired of it and fought back. Nowadays, they're just fightin' to keep the white man off'n their homelands." Tatum motioned around them and pointed to the different mountain ranges. "This here is gettin' in the territory of the Utes, and o'er yonder where we are and further south, that's Comanche. Now down yonder," pointing to the south end of the valley, "That's Jicarilla Apache. Ain't met up with them yet, seen a few of 'em last hunt, but ain't met 'em. Ain't met the Ute, neither. But most Indians ain't no different from us. Just people that want their own freedom and their own homes and families and to be left alone."

Joseph gazed into the fire and tried to absorb all that Tatum had said. Just the thought that all people, no matter the color, were basically the same, was new to him. With a lifetime of being told they were less than the white man and only useful for labor, this thought that he was as good as others was a pleasing thought and one he wanted to ponder on. He was brought from his reverie with the rising of Tatum, who went to get the bedrolls so they could turn in for the night.

As they lay looking up at the stars on this clear night, Tatum said, "Tomorrow, we'll roll out early and see if we can find any of the buffalo that might still be around. I saw some fresh sign down near the creek and we might be lucky enough to get a couple as they come to water."

With his hands behind his head, Joseph looked at the diamond studded canopy and said, "My, my, them stars sho' is beautiful. I never thought I'd be so close to 'em. It's like lookin' into Heaven."

Tatum chuckled and said, "I'm sure Heaven is even prettier than that."

CHAPTER FIFTEEN
UTE

THE SMALL COOKFIRE CAST A LONG SHADOW AS TATUM HUNKERED over the flames grabbing at the warmth and waiting for the coffee to perk. The first snow of the winter season left no more than a few inches of light fluffy flakes that sparkled in the firelight. First snows were usually dry and light, holding little moisture to wet the flats. Tatum had to brush off the long log at fire's edge for a dry seat. The remaining stars of the early morning held tight to the blanket of night, refusing to give way to the rising sun. Tatum coughed when the tendril of smoke curled under his hat brim and he choked as he waved the smoke away. Joseph was wakened by the coughing and grumbling of his friend and he slowly rolled from the comforting warmth of the blankets. He stood and stretched, walked to the nearby cluster of sage to tend to his morning needs and walked back to the fire stretching his galluses over his shoulders.

Tatum poured two cups of steaming coffee and nodded as he muttered, "Mornin'," to Joseph.

Joseph looked around in the dim light, turned to look to the slight grey that silhouetted the distant Sangre ridge and replied, "Looks to me to still be night."

Tatum chuckled and said, "I'm thinkin' if we wanna get them

buffler, we need to head out on foot, work our way up this side of the creek and see if we can catch 'em 'fore they start wanderin'."

"Sounds good, but I ain't never shot no buff'lo 'fore," replied Joseph.

"Well, I was thinkin' 'bout that. Since your flintlock ain't very big, maybe you could take my Hawken. You can shoot straight, can'tchu?"

"Yassuh, I be a purty good shot wit' 'bout anythin'," answered Joseph.

"I'll use my longbow an' you can back me up with the Hawken. I ain't interested in announcin' our presence to the Ute that live in this country, so, if I take it with my longbow we might make a kill and get outta here without them even knowin' we were here," surmised Tatum. "But if he don't go down, you might need to finish it off with the Hawken. If you do, then we'll need to make short work of dressin' it out and gettin' away."

"Whatever you say, fine wid me," replied Joseph.

They finished their coffee, tossing the dregs aside and upending their cups on the rocks, and readied themselves for the hunt. With the horses and mules tethered, their camp secured with packs and gear stashed by the trees, they started out. Tatum led the way, holding to the flank of the rolling hills to the north of the creek, leaving a sparse trail in the fresh snow. The serpentine creek, with occasional beaver ponds, fed the willows and alder bushes that marked the banks. Away from the tangle of willows, patches of dusty green held grasses that were the favored feeding of the buffalo and where Tatum hoped to find some of the tasty humpbacks grazing.

As they walked, the valley closed ranks and narrowed the creek bottom. The thick growths of brush commandeered the flat-bottomed valley and the willows were humbled by the fresh snow, but Tatum looked farther upstream and the with the grey light of morning giving way to the rosy cast of sunrise, he saw the valley opening wide and revealing a white flat with several dark forms slowly moving about. As they neared, he was cautious to shield their presence by slowly moving among the sparse juniper, and he saw the valley split with the main branch of the creek taking a wide bend to the north and another fork bearing to the west. But his concern was focused on the grazing buffalo, now two hundred yards away. He whispered to Joseph, "Let's move back a ways and drop down by the creek. I think the willows will give us more cover and we can get closer."

Joseph answered by turning to retrace their steps among the juniper and pinyon to the point where the valley narrowed and they could retreat to the willows without being seen. The buffalo were stirring around, searching for graze near the creekbank and the willows, digging in the shallow snow, brushing it away with their snouts, and Tatum noticed they seemed to be nervous about something, but he didn't think they had spotted him. The wind was in their favor, a slight breeze coming down the valley from behind the buffalo and into the face of the hunters, and he knew the buffalo's eyesight was such that they had not given away their location behind the willows.

"We only need one good sized buffler, an' I'd as soon take it with my longbow. We're in Ute country and I don't want to alarm them with a rifle shot. But you stand ready, just in case," whispered Tatum to Joseph, as he eyed the wary beasts.

"Just in case what?" asked Joseph.

"Anything, maybe the buffler will charge us, or some injuns hear us. Just be ready," he warned.

They were within less than one hundred yards, when suddenly the heads of the grazing animals jerked up as they looked to their rear. There were more buffalo than Tatum had first counted, but the entire herd bolted and started at a run down the valley toward the open flats of the larger valley below. The ground shook, the snow billowed, and dust rose, and the swaying bulbous wooly heads with lolling tongues swinging about, formed an ominous beast that seemed to be charging as one. Tatum shouted to Joseph, "Down! Below the bank! They won't see us!"

The two men dropped below the edge of the bank behind the cover of willows, snow shaking from above searched for bare necks and Tatum watched. He suddenly stood up, bow bent with the nocked arrow, and he let fly the dart of death between the branches of the willow as the herd of about a hundred woolies thundered by. He watched the arrow find its mark as he blindly nocked another and sent it to find the other. The big beast stumbled and went to its knees plowing a furrow with its chin. Then Tatum saw the cause of the stampede. In close pursuit were about twenty Ute warriors with upraised lances and bows as they rode alongside their targets. With warriors screaming and shouting, buffalo bellowing and roaring, dirt and dust billowing, the mass of buffalo and hunters thundered past the two astounded men. They watched as the herd and hunters continued into the flats of the valley.

Tatum looked as the snowy dust cloud settled and saw several downed beasts before them. He knew there would be others from the Ute village that would soon converge on the scene and he deliberated what they should do, determined not to lose the buffalo he had downed. Still behind the willows and not easily seen, he stood and surveyed the kill area. Then looking upstream to the fork of the valley, he saw several women and children coming, several leading horses with travois, all anxious to get to the fresh kills. As he waited, he also saw some of the hunters returning from down valley, and he watched as they were met by the butchering crew. With most Indians, the job of butchering was left to the women, but the men would often take the first cut of the carcass and enjoy the fresh liver dipped in bile. As he observed the hunters pointing out their kills, known by the arrows or lances still embedded in the carcasses, he saw one warrior, apparently a leader of some sort, sitting his horse beside the cow killed by Tatum's arrows. He was looking at the arrows, knowing they were different, and started to look around.

Tatum stepped from the willows, bow in hand with arrow nocked, and started toward his kill. The warrior spotted him immediately and brought his bow up, but seeing Tatum's bow at his side unthreatening, lowered his as well. Tatum walked to the downed buffalo, took his nocked arrow and extended it to the warrior. He struggled to remove the arrows from the carcass, having to cut them free, and handed them to the warrior as well. The Indian looked at Tatum, then at each of the arrows, and holding them in his left hand, he retrieved one of his with his right, laid it alongside Tatum's, and saw the white man's arrows were a handbreadth longer and the fletching was longer, and the points were metal. He nodded as he compared the arrows, grunted and handed Tatum's arrows back to him.

Tatum said, "I am Tate Saint, or Longbow as I am known among other tribes."

"You make home in mountains," said the warrior, pointing to the Sangres.

Tatum lifted his head, smiled, and said, "You know of us?"

"I am Two Eagles, of the Caputa Ute. I am the Warchief. You are Longbow?" he asked, motioning to the bow in Tatum's hand.

"Yes, I am known as Longbow. It is a name given to me by the Kiowa chief, Dohäsan," he turned and looked to the willows where Joseph waited, motioning for him to come out, "and this is my friend, Joseph Thomas."

Two Eagles watched Joseph come from the willows and the surprise at seeing a black man was evident on his face. He looked at Tatum and back at Joseph and said, "I have heard of these men that look like a buffalo, but I have never seen one before."

Joseph walked as casually as he dared, cradling the Hawken in his arms across his chest. He had never been this close to any Indian and he didn't know what to expect, but he trusted Tatum. He was bare-headed, and Two Eagles looked at his hair, gigged his horse nearer and reached out to touch it, but Joseph drew back. Tatum scowled and motioned for the boy to let the chief touch his hair. Joseph straightened up and looked sideways as the warrior slowly moved his hand across his hair.

The chief looked at Tatum and said, "Feels like buffalo," and reined his horse back from the two men. Other warriors had drawn up nearby and watched as their chief dealt with the two strangers.

Two Eagles looked back at the willows and said, "You have no women to butcher your kill?"

"We do, but not with us. We will take it back to our cabin and let them take care of it there," explained Tatum, knowing the warriors placed great stock in the different duties of men and women. Any man that did not have a woman to do his work was considered less than a man, as Tatum had learned from his earlier stay with the Comanche. He added, "They are back at the cabin, preparing our meat for the winter."

Two Eagles slowly nodded his head in understanding although his expression showed doubt. His scouts had told him of this man and his Comanche squaw, but he did not know of this buffalo man. He looked at the white man, surprised his chosen weapon for buffalo was a bow, and motioned as he spoke, "You choose the bow to hunt. It is hard to take a buffalo with a bow, and from the ground. That looks like it is too big to use from a horse, is it not so?"

Tatum lifted the bow and said, "Yes, it would be hard to use from a horse. But it has more power than other bows and I killed this buffalo with two arrows."

Two Eagles looked at the man, the bow, and the carcass, nodding his head slowly. He knew it was hard to make a kill shot on a running buffalo even when riding alongside and close in, and to make a kill shot while standing, and especially to put two arrows close to one another and both in the kill area of a running buffalo, was an extraordinary feat. This was a man to be respected, he knew of few warriors that could duplicate this skill. He looked at Joseph and said, "You did not shoot?"

"No suh, we only needed one, so, I don' need ta shoot," explained Joseph.

Again, Two Eagles nodded his head in understanding and respect for men that chose to kill only what they needed.

"You will join us for our feast. When the butchering is done, the women will start cooking and we will eat. You will join us."

It came across as more of a command than an invitation and Tatum considered, looked at the carcass, and said, "We will join you."

Tatum had always freely given respect and showed deference to others and it served him well. Circumstances, that could be argued by most as extraordinary, had somehow repeatedly placed him in close contact with several different groups of Indians, and each time he had gained their respect and became friends with each tribe. He hoped this would be another profitable time as he sought friendship with the Ute people. Joseph left to retrieve the horses and mules and Tatum looked at the sky, wondering if they would be in for more snow, and turned to the work of butchering the big cow buffalo.

CHAPTER SIXTEEN
TAKEN

WHITE FEATHER AND LIZZIE HAD GROWN CLOSE IN THE tutor/student relationship, yet both thought of it closer to mother/daughter. Yet with less than a decade between them, their friendship and mutual dependence grew. The first day of Tatum and Joseph's hunt saw the women finishing the storing of prepared meat and making additional drying racks. In the afternoon, White Feather showed her skill at weaving alder roots and willow withes into a tight basket. She explained that after their gathering of the berries and plants, she would show Lizzie how to make the basket watertight with tree sap. Every new lesson learned, and skill garnered increased the confidence of the previously shy and withdrawn Lizzie. She was blossoming under the tutelage and friendship of White Feather and the older woman was enjoying sharing her wilderness knowledge.

"As soon as we are done here, we'll use your new bow and practice some. You are getting very good and you will soon be able to use it to hunt," explained White Feather.

"Oh, you think so? I'm mighty glad, cuz I need to get good so I can help my brother," answered Lizzie.

"Among my people, many women do not go hunting. But some, like me, choose to hunt and go into battle."

"You mean you fight with the men?" asked Lizzie, aghast at the revelation.

"As I grew, I would practice with my brother and his friends, and I became as good as any of them. I have hunted, and I have gone into battle," shared White Feather. "That is how I broke my leg, I was chasing a buffalo and my horse stepped in a prairie dog hole and threw me. Tatum pulled me from the place so I did not get trampled by the buffalo."

"Oh, my, sounds like he save yo' life!" exclaimed Lizzie.

White Feather nodded her head as she smiled, remembering. "I would have returned to my village, but you and your brother needed to be cared for, so I stayed."

"Oh, I thought you an' Tate were . . . you know . . . together," stumbled Lizzie, trying not to ask the obvious question.

"We are friends. He helped my people so now I help him. It was good to be here and help him heal."

"Well, now that he's purty healed up, you gonna stay or go?"

"We are preparing for winter," answered White Feather, noncommittally. She turned away from question she had wondered about herself.

The target fashioned by White Feather was a hoop with the stretched skin of a prairie dog. She hung it from a low branch of the tall ponderosa at the edge of their camp and walked back to Lizzie. She picked up her own bow, nocked an arrow and let it fly, hitting the target near the center. As the target swung back and forth from the impact of the arrow, White Feather turned to Lizzie, nodded and pointed for the girl to take her shot. Within a few seconds, the target hung totally still with the arrow hanging at an awkward angle, and Lizzie brought up her bow, drew the arrow back and with her thumb at her cheek and sighting along the shaft, she let it fly and it whispered to the target, striking next to the arrow of White Feather. Lizzie jumped for joy and White Feather grinned at the antics of the girl, but walked to retrieve their arrows. As she stood near the suspended target, she withdrew the arrows and stepped slightly to the side and called to Lizzie, "I will let the target swing, you hit it while it is moving." She watched as the girl nocked an arrow and lifted her bow, then she pulled the target to one side and let go so it would swing side to side. She stepped farther to the side to be free of the target area and nodded at Lizzie, who immediately loosed an arrow. It was a clean miss. White Feather again went to the target and instructed Lizzie, "Time your shot, allow for the flight of the arrow, and let it go when the target is well back from your sight."

The girl nodded, and White Feather again started the target swinging, and stepped to the side. This time the arrow flew true and took the target at the edge as it swung aside. White Feather nodded, gave additional encouragement and instruction and set for another try. By the time dusk pulled the light from the sky, Lizzie was hitting the target with every shot, much to the approval of White Feather. The women returned to the fire and sat with a warm cup of coffee and visited, sharing stories of each other's youth.

WHEN THE WOMEN exited the cabin in the early light of morning, they were surprised to see the fresh dusting of snow. Although no more than an inch or so, the quiet and softness of the morning was made more so with the blanket of white. Lizzie marveled at the beauty of the pine trees that held the light fluffy flakes, and the purity of the snow covered clearing and the trails that were obscured, leaving no trace of man or beast.

"Oh, it's so beautiful!" she whispered as if not wanting the beauty to leave with the sound of her voice.

White Feather smiled at the innocence of the girl, moved past her to gather some wood and start a fire. As she looked back at Lizzie, she said, "Enjoy it. It will be gone shortly, and you won't even know it came."

They quickly finished their morning meal and started on the day's task of gathering additional stores for the winter. Both women carried their bows, quivers full of arrows at their sides, and watched for any game that could be taken. With the sun rising over the Sangres and casting long shadows with the pines, the women walked in the shade, kicking their way through the drifted snow. The wind had cleared much of the flats, piling the light snow on the lee side of the bushes and willows. White Feather spotted a trail of a big snowshoe leading behind a large cluster of sage and pointed it out to Lizzie. With hand signals she told the younger woman to be ready for the rabbit to come out the left side, and White Feather picked up a couple of stones, walked closer to the brush and began pelting it with rocks. Instantly the long-eared big-footed bundle of fur sprang from cover and leaped toward the willows, but Lizzie's arrow caught it mid-flight and brought it to the ground, still kicking at the snow. White Feather snatched it up by the ears and turned with a smile to Lizzie, holding the trophy high.

"Good! You did good!" praised White Feather.

"It skeered me! I ain't neva' seen one wid' ears like that!" replied Lizzie.

"There are smaller rabbits, but these are called snowshoes, because of their big feet!" explained White Feather as she walked back to Lizzie. She pointed out the fur, saying, "They have grown their winter coats, and will make good for our moccasins."

By mid-afternoon, the snow had melted or blown away, the ground was dry and the women had bagged four snowshoe rabbits and gathered two baskets full of shoots, sprouts, roots, berries, and plants for winter stores. They had enjoyed the profitable time together and were walking alongside the willows at creekside, heads down, laughing and talking. As they rounded a large clump of willows beside one of the few beaver ponds, they were brought up suddenly by a group of waiting warriors.

No one moved, but Lizzie surreptitiously felt for the bow, now unstrung and in the quiver with her arrows, as White Feather barked a warning in a language Lizzie had not heard.

"What do you want? Why are the Apache here? Do you have to

come so far from your land to find something to eat? Are you not good enough hunters to find food where you live?"

White Feather spoke in Jicarilla Apache, an Athabascan guttural language, but she was fluent, and the warriors stood unmoving before her insults.

"Are you such mighty warriors and hunters that you have to take a few rabbits from women?" she continued, gesticulating and shouting with a ferocity to her voice and her facial expression.

Lizzie was afraid and surprised at White Feather's reaction. Although she couldn't understand the older woman's words, her expressions told of her meaning. Lizzie remained frozen in place, waiting for some movement or word from White Feather. Finally, one of the men, an apparent leader, stepped forward, waved his arm angrily and shouting to his men, stirring them to action. Within a few short moments, the men, eight of them, had tackled the women, disarmed them and bound their arms behind them.

The leader, a stocky man, slightly shorter than most, but broader and more muscular with a flat nose, long black hair held back from his eyes with a cloth headband, and knee-high moccasins and a breech-cloth, stepped forward and with quick motions, directed his men to lift the women to their feet and stand them before him. White Feather scowled at her captor and the man stepped before her with his face no more than inches away and snarled, "I am Crazy Wolf, and you are my captives. You will do as you are told, or I will gladly slit your throat from ear to ear."

White Feather spat in his face and he stumbled backwards, then sprang forward and backhanded the Comanche across her face, making her fall to her knees beside Lizzie. He spat at her and looked to Lizzie, who stared back with wide eyes, but remained silent. He muttered something to her, which she did not understand but thought it was some kind of threat of violence, and she nodded her head nervously, seeking to allay any assault. White Feather cautioned, "Don't say anything," as she struggled to her feet.

Ba'iitso, as his warriors called him, motioned to his men to bring the women. Two men slipped rawhide thongs over their heads and around their throats, pulling them tight, and swung aboard their horses, tugging on the rawhide to pull the women behind them. The women, first with long strides, then at a trot, struggled to keep up with the warriors riding horseback. Their bounty of rabbits, bows and arrows, were taken by another man that followed behind, occasionally goading them by pushing his horse to bump them. Whenever one of the women stumbled and fell the watching warriors laughed as the fallen struggled to get to her feet before being drug by the neck.

The lateness of the hour and the soon darkening skies worked to the advantage of the women and forced the men to make camp before they were exhausted. They were bound to a pair of aspen at the edge of the camp while the men prepared their rabbits for their own meal. Lizzie asked, "Who are they? And what are they going to do with us?"

"They are Jicarilla Apache, and they are not known for treating captives kindly," answered White Feather, as she spat in their direction.

CHAPTER SEVENTEEN
PURSUIT

THE FEAST WITH THE CAPUTA UTE AFTER THE HUNT WAS A GOOD time. Two Eagles' woman, Red Bird, prepared the part of the feast for the warrior chief and those of his choosing. Among those gathered by their cookfire were Cloud Dancer, the Shaman of the village, and Coyote Running, who seemed to be the jokester of the group. Coyote was always smiling and usually laughing, making fun of everything and everyone. Tatum thought it unusual for any warrior to have the name coyote. Most native people considered the coyote a trickster and deceiver and would usually not put that name on any of their offspring, but the more time spent with this man, the more the name fit. Just his antics took the tension from the gathering and everyone seemed to relax and enjoy the time together.

Two Eagles was especially interested in Joseph and quizzed him about his life and was surprised to learn of his slavery. "I was told that a slave would always be a slave and could not change. But you are here and are no longer a slave, that is good." His comments called for an explanation and Joseph told of his life and the flight of his family to find a place of freedom. Two Eagles responded, "There is freedom in our world, but there is also slavery. When a captive is taken, he is considered the same as a slave and can be traded, used or sacrificed. Few ever escape and find freedom."

It was a somber note and caused Joseph to lapse into deep thought, comparing his life as a slave and the real possibility of never finding true freedom with slavery all around, even among the native tribes. Tatum changed the conversation and spoke of making his home in the Sangres and how he hoped to be at peace with the Ute people. Two Eagles replied, "It is good for us to be at peace. You have shown yourself to be a man of truth and peace, your home is between the land of the Comanche and the Ute. My people will consider you a friend and will be at peace with you. If you come to our village, you will be welcome."

"Thank you, Two Eagles. Maybe one day soon we," and motioned to Joseph and himself, "will bring the women with us and visit your village. Perhaps we can trade and learn more of each other's ways." Two Eagles grinned, nodding his head in understanding and agreement.

The men stood and clasped forearms and said their goodbyes. Two Eagles was surprised these men chose to travel at night, but understood their desire to be home. They had packed the buffalo meat in the paniers and packs on the mules and swung aboard their mounts, bid the Ute goodbye and started out with the North Star at their backs. The moon was waxing into the third quarter and the clear night made the travel easy. They were determined to travel as far and as fast as the stamina of the horses and mules would allow.

With two short rest stops, one well after midnight and the other shortly after the break of day, they neared the homesite with the animals trudging quietly on the carpet of pine needles that covered the trail to the cabin. There was an unusual quietness, the silence that portends the absence of life. Tatum reined up while well back in the trees, slipped the Hawken from the scabbard under his leg, checked the load and cap, cocked the hammer and laid the rifle across his legs and the pommel of the saddle. He nodded to Joseph, who mimicked his actions with his own rifle, and Tatum nudged his mount forward to the clearing. As they entered, nothing moved. There was an absence of birds and other varmints that provided the underlying course of sounds, no breeze stirred the branches of trees, even the nearby aspen that stubbornly clung to the last of the golden leaves, stood still. It was the kind of silence that almost forbid breathing and for a few moments, Tatum did not.

He quietly slipped from his saddle, handed the reins to Joseph, checked his Paterson loosing it in his holster, and started for the cabin door. He pushed it open, looked into the dim light and saw bedrolls on the bed frames, but no sign of the women. He turned and walked to the lean-to that extended from the overhang and then to the cave entrance, finding no sign of the women and no fresh track made that day. He walked back to Joseph and took the reins of his mount and spoke to Joseph, "There's no sign of them. Let's put the animals in the corral, put up the meat and if they're still not back, we'll go looking."

Joseph replied, "Yassuh, that sounds right," and stepped down from the big bay and went to the corral to open the gate and lead the mules in to start de-rigging the animals. They stacked the bundles of meat in the cave on the newly made racks, returned the heavy door to cover the entry and went to the wickiup to stow the rest of the gear. Taking their time in hopes of the soon return of the women, the duties were soon finished, and they looked at one another with the understanding they needed to start their search.

"Look, they were only looking for rabbits and berries and such, and the only place for that is along the creek in the bottom yonder. You head upstream, and I'll go downstream a ways, we'll work back this way lookin' for them or any sign and we'll meet here by the rocks," referring to a promontory that extended into the valley floor and was marked with several large boulder formations. "If you find somethin' important, or find them hurt or somethin', just fire a shot and the other'n'll come runnin', got that?"

"Yassuh, sho' do. How fah' ya' think we oughta go?" asked Joseph.

"Oh, a mile or so, whatever seems right, you know, by the lay of the land and such," answered Tatum. Joseph looked at him questioningly, but remained silent though wondering at his remark.

They chose to make the first search on foot, knowing they could cover ample territory and have a better chance at spotting any sign of the women's passing. They trotted off to their chosen locations to begin the search and were soon out of sight of one another. Joseph dropped from the trees and through the scattered juniper and pinyon of the lower shoulders of the mountain, and trotted across the sage covered flat to gain the grassy sloping creek bank. He scanned the area and seeing nothing, started at a dog-trot downstream, searching the willows, the creek, and the sage clusters for any sign of the women. He had gone just a short distance and he almost stepped in the remains of a small gut-pile from one of the rabbits taken by the women. He dropped to one knee and scanned the area, spotting several moccasin tracks, but could easily tell by the blown debris in the tracks, and the absence of any moisture, that the tracks were from the day before. He stood, looked around, and resumed his quick pace downstream.

It was less than a quarter hour later when Tatum and Joseph met at the rocks. Joseph was excited to tell Tatum about the sign of several rabbit kills and what little was left of the remains after the coyotes feasted. He finished with, "But all the tracks was from yestiddy, nothin' fresh."

Tatum had patiently listened to Joseph's report and dropped his head as he began to tell of his findings.

"Well, from what I can tell, just a short way back yonder, they ran into a bunch of Indians. Don't know what kind, but it 'pears they been took."

"Took, whatchu' mean, took?" asked Joseph frantically.

"Just that. From what I can make out, the bunch of Indians caught 'em, bound 'em, and made 'em follow 'long behind. The Indians were all mounted, but they made the women walk."

"Well, where are dey? Where'd dey go?" pleaded Joseph.

Tatum motioned for Joseph to settle down, "Settle down, settle down, we're goin' after 'em. Now, come on up to the cabin, we'll get ready. But we need to give the animals a bit more rest, pack us up some grub, and I'm thinkin' we'll have 'nuff light we can foller 'em a ways tonite."

Joseph led the way to the cabin, his long strides making Tatum break into a trot to keep up. Tatum went first to the cavern for a good supply of smoked meat, knowing that when traveling fast, it was best to have food that can be consumed on the move. Joseph put together a few other supplies from the cabin, that would be needed and appreciated when they had to stop for the night and desired a better meal. He checked his own supply of powder and balls, extra powder and lead was packed, and percussion caps for the Hawken and Paterson. With arms full of supplies he exited the cabin and was brought up short with the presence of three mounted Indians in the clearing. Tatum was speaking with one man and Joseph slowly dropped the supplies and waited.

When Tatum heard the approach of horses, he stepped back behind the corner of the cabin, Hawken in hand, and waited. When the horsemen cleared the timber, he immediately recognized Raven, the brother of White Feather, and stepped away from the cabin, motioning the riders to come into the clearing.

"Greetings my brother," said Tatum in the language of the Comanche.

"Greetings to you," answered Raven. "We have come for White Feather," he stated as he looked around for his sister. Behind him was Tall Elk, the one-time suitor of White Feather that had been shunned by the woman, but who never gave up on the her. He had been determined to have her for his own and it was at his insistence that Raven make this trip to bring White Feather back to the village. Now he too searched the clearing for White Feather.

Tatum spoke up, "Well, I'm glad you came and at the right time. We just returned from a hunt and discovered the women, White Feather and Lizzie, have been taken."

Raven turned to face Tatum and with fire in his eyes asked, "Taken? Who has taken my sister?"

"Well, I'm not rightly sure. From the tracks, I'd say a group of Indians, maybe ten or so, took the women yesterday, 'bout this time. We were just getting ready to go after 'em, and you're sure welcome to come with us."

"Where were they taken?" asked Raven, still showing alarm in his eyes.

"Right down yonder, just some little ways downstream from thar," Tatum pointed toward the promontory of rocks, "the tracks are purty plain."

Raven motioned to Tall Elk and Big Belly to go to the place and search out the tracks. They quickly left to do as bidden and Raven looked at Tatum and asked, "Are you ready?"

"Purt'near. I'll get our horses and we'll get loaded up. If'n you wanna go 'head on, we'll catch up."

Raven looked at the white man, nodded his head, and nudged his horse away and trotted down to the flats and the creek. Tatum and Joseph hurriedly loaded the pack mule, caught up their horses and saddled up, stepped up, and started out. Tatum looked at the sky, nodded approvingly at the blue and knowing the night would be clear. He hoped they would make good time in their pursuit.

When they caught up with Raven, he told them, "Jicarilla, they have been taken by the Apache. That is not good, they are our enemies. There are twelve, but they are not moving too fast, probably because of the women."

"Wal, we're figgerin' on keepin' after 'em tonight. There'll be good moonlight and we might make up some ground on 'em."

Raven looked at the white man, surprised at his determination to travel even at night. "Do you think you can track them?" asked Raven.

"Probably not as good as you can. You're comin' ain'tcha?" asked Tatum.

Raven lifted his head and said, "We will ride together."

CHAPTER EIGHTEEN
SIGN

THE UNCOMFORTABLE NIGHT WAS SPENT HUGGING THE SMOOTH BARK of the aspens. The women had their hands tied together after their arms were stretched around the white barked trunks. What sleep they got came in short snatches, until their weight cut off the circulation in their arms and brought a throbbing pain. There was little to be said, they already concluded there was little chance of rescue and silence suited their mood of despair.

Questions went unanswered and the possibility of escape seemed beyond their grasp. But their weariness forced them to snooze, even though their discomfort fought against it. It was the time when the eastern sky just showed a hint of light, when a sudden kick to her hip wakened White Feather with a start. She looked up to see the squat figure of Crazy Wolf grinning at her. His face was illuminated by the stirring coals of the cookfire and appeared even more menacing than the day before. He let a sinister laugh escape as he looked at his captive.

"You will ride with Spotted Pony, the ch'eekéé will ride with me. I have not seen one so dark before, what tribe is she from?" asked the burly figure, now squatting on his heels beside White Feather.

"She is what the Magáanii call a negro," explained White Feather.

The Apache often used Spanish in their trades at Sante Fe and Taos and knew the word negro was the same as the Spanish term meaning black. "I will call her Poco Buffalo. You I give to Bear Killer, the leader of our band of Abáachi mizaa," explained Crazy Wolf. He quickly stood and strode away to the campfire. The conversation had awakened Lizzie and she asked, "What was that about?"

"He said he was taking you as his woman, you will be called Little Buffalo, and he is giving me to the chief of their band, a man called Bear Killer."

"His woman!? What does that mean?"

"We will not walk, we will ride. You will ride with him," she answered evasively. Although by white men's standards, Lizzie would be considered a little young to become a wife, among the plains Indians she was of the right age. White Feather didn't want to alarm Lizzie, but she knew the girl would not be treated kindly by either the Apache people or Crazy Wolf. She would be nothing more than a slave, and would be expected to serve her master in any way he demanded.

The women were untied and led to the horses where Spotted Pony and Crazy Wolf waited. Both men were mounted and reached down for the women, lifting them by their bound wrists to set the women behind them. Crazy Wolf turned and dropped a rawhide loop over Lizzie's head and drew it tight around her neck. He held the end of the rawhide in his hand and warned her with motions, not to try to get free or she would choke. White Feather was secured in a similar fashion and the two men led the group from the trees, following a well-used game trail to the flanks of the Sangres, bearing to the South. Midday saw them turning to west and following the Trinchera creek that cut across the flats of the San Luis valley.

With nothing to eat since their capture, the women were growing weak and had to hold tight to their captors. The rocking gait of the horses continued, and the tired women dozed against the men until the hunting party reined away from the creek to a cluster of juniper on the flank of a group of mounds that stood as lonesome sentinels over the flats. Everyone dismounted, and the women were dropped near the fire ring hastily assembled by the men. One man brought a hind quarter of a deer and sliced off portions for the men to cook for their meal. Spotted Pony placed several slices on a flat rock tilted toward the flames. He looked at White Feather and Lizzie, pointed to the meat and motioned to his mouth indicating they were to eat. The raw meat was barely heated through when White Feather snatched two slices, handing one to Lizzie. The girl looked at the meat, wrinkled her nose as she looked at White Feather and back at the meat. White Feather was busy chewing and savoring the first food since their capture. She looked at Lizzie and said, "You must eat, you may not get anything for days, eat!" Lizzie bit into it, tore off a bite and began to chew. The hunger overcame her revulsion at the raw meat and it soon disappeared.

The south facing slope caught the midday sun and the full bellies of the Apache gave them an excuse to let the horses rest while they took a short nap in the warm sun. Lizzie and White Feather stretched out side by side and soon dozed off. But it seemed like just a few moments and they were drug to their feet as the hunting party gathered their horses and started back on the trail. It was less than an hour later when Crazy Wolf stopped, holding up a hand for the men behind. The Trinchera creek they followed was a twisty winding creek and often flanked by willows, alder and many berry bushes, all enticing food for deer and antelope. Wolf had spotted three deer, two does and a yearling, eating chokecherries from the brush and so occupied with their feast, they had not seen nor heard the approach of the hunting party. With hand signals, Wolf directed his men to stalk the deer from among the willows, he and Spotted Pony slipped from their mounts and stayed with the women and the horses.

Within moments, the men had the busy deer within range of their bows and arrows and at a hand signal, arrows whispered to their mark and all three animals sprang up in alarm, tried to escape but staggered and fell, each impaled by at least two arrows. The successful hunters shouted for joy and the party quickly converged on the carcasses. In short order, the deer were fully dressed, with the heads, legs and entrails removed, but leaving the hides on the carcasses. At Crazy Wolf's direction, their pack horses were brought forward and loaded with the meat, secured, and the party was again on their way. The entire occurrence took no more than half an hour.

The women had no idea how far they would travel, but White Feather knew the party was showing their anticipation at reaching the village soon. The sun was beginning to drop behind the distant San Juan mountains when the party came to the banks of a wide river. White Feather knew this to be the Rio Grande, telling Lizzie she thought they would soon be to the village. The muddy water had carved a wide bend from the sandy banks and the far side showed an expansive shore of smooth sand. Crazy Wolf did not hesitate as they approached the water, nudging his horse into the slow-moving current, causing Lizzie to grab tighter to the rawhide belt of the man. The shallow water came to the belly of the horses, but the crossing was easy and without incident, and each of the horses did their customary shake to free themselves of the excess water, startling Lizzie. When she gasped with a muted shriek, Wolf laughed at her surprise with a deep rumbling chuckle. He said something in Apache which Lizzie figured was an insult of some kind, but she didn't let on she had any idea.

Lizzie was dressed in a long buckskin tunic made by White Feather, and sitting astraddle of the horse, her legs were bare from above the knee to her high-topped moccasins. Twice, Wolf had put his fingers on her leg, rubbing as if he were trying to remove some-thing, then looked at his hand, apparently to see if any of the color came off on his hand. Each time he shook his head in wonder, but Lizzie was disgusted at his touch, and repeatedly flinched, but she could not move away from him.

Crazy Wolf would often stop and scan their back trail, but the thinking of the Apache was there were only two men, one a magáanii, or white man, that would follow.

Ba'iitso, Crazy Wolf, knew he could easily take the magáanii any time he wanted. But the thought of the haskįįyįį łizhįį, or the black man, was somewhat unsettling. He thought of the Apache ceremonies where the men would impersonate the Gans, or mountain spirits, by dressing in black masks and performing the dance rituals seeking to dispel the bad spirits, and he wondered if this ch'eekée, or girl with the dark skin and the haskįįyįį łizhįį, were really some of the mountain spirits in the flesh.

By the time the sun had dropped below the horizon and the dim light of twilight covered the land, White Feather saw the glow of campfires among the trees. Beyond the village, a rocky butte rose and gave the appearance of a sheltering god with outstretched arms holding a blanket of protection, and Feather would soon learn this was Sierro del Ojito, or the mount of the overlook. She only hoped that the image of protection would hold true for her and Lizzie, but she was afraid they would not be welcomed and would probably soon have a greater sense of regret than ever before since the day of their capture.

CHAPTER NINETEEN
TRACKING

DARK WOLF WAS A PROVEN TRACKER, HIS FELLOW WARRIORS WOULD brag that Dark Wolf could track an eagle across the sky. He scouted the trail, following the Apache. Although an excellent reader of sign, Dark Wolf had never attempted to track anything in the dim moonlight and was challenged to keep to the trail. But the moon was waxing close to full and the cloudless night worked to the favor of the tracker as did the carelessness of the arrogant Apache, believing that if anyone followed, they would pose no real threat. The Apache had intentionally left an easy trail, anticipating that if the two men followed, the warriors could easily win more honors and take more scalps.

Dark Wolf reined up beside a cluster of juniper that shielded the stream from view, the chuckle of the water over the rocks added music to the still night. He waited for the others and within moments he saw Raven and Longbow ride into the open, coming to him.

"They do not try to hide their trail, I believe they want to be caught. They may wait to ambush us," said Dark Wolf to Raven as he pointed to the clear tracks crossing the small creek.

"They do not know we are here. They think it is only Longbow and his friend, the black one. If we can overtake them before they reach their village, maybe we can get the women back," said Raven, speaking to both Dark Wolf and Tatum. "But, if they reach the village before we find them, there will be too many for us."

Tatum remained silent, thinking about the possibilities of rescuing the women and the probability of not reaching them in time. He didn't want to think of what would happen to the women in the hands of the Apache, although he did not know much of the Jicarilla ways, both White Feather and Raven told of their cruelty to enemies and the eagerness of the Apache to go into battle. All he could do was to hope and pray they would be in time. He looked at the starlit sky and noticed a gathering of clouds to the west over the San Juans and hoped they were not snow clouds. That would be all they needed, to be caught in the open in a blizzard that would wipe out any tracks of the Apache.

Raven motioned for Dark Wolf to continue to scout the trail ahead and waved to the others to follow as he nudged his horse forward. The clatter of hooves on stone and the splashing of water told of the crossing of the small creek and Tatum pulled the collar of the Hudson Bay capote around his neck, seeking to stay the chill air. He remembered when Carson had suggested that he trade for the Capote, telling him, "You ain't known cold till you feel the bite of winter comin' off them mountains, no sir. The best thing you can have is a good wool coat." Now with the bite of winter gnawing at Tatum's flesh, he was glad he heeded the mountain man's advice. He looked at Joseph with the heavy blanket around his shoulders, held together by one hand while he struggled with the lead rope of the pack mule and the reins of his horse with the other. The Comanche had buffalo robes around their shoulders, except for Dark Wolf, who rode with nothing to cut the cold but a buckskin shirt.

It was well before dawn when Dark Wolf signaled them to stop. The wind had picked up and the cloud cover and beginning of snow was making the tracking difficult. He had chosen a campsite on the lee side of a small butte with enough of an overhang to give shelter from the snow and wind and making a fire possible. With the wind coming from the west and the trail leading directly into the wind, the fire on the back side of the butte would not be easily seen and would be welcomed by the five men and their animals. Orders were unnecessary as everyone took to their tasks, knowing the animals needed picketing, firewood gathered, and cover provided. Within moments the men were huddled against the sandstone wall of the overhang as the fire kept the cold at bay, reflecting the heat from the wall and adding to the warmth of the robes and blankets used by the men.

By full light, the horses and mule stood hipshot facing the sandstone face of the bluff and the men were stirring in their blankets and robes. And the snowstorm continued unabated although the wind had calmed leaving the white curtain of big flakes to cover the grass and cactus of the flats. The heavy snow had already accumulated to a handbreadth and at the current rate, it would soon reach a foot and make travel more difficult.

As Tatum rolled from his blankets, he stood and stretched, almost reaching the ceiling of the overhang with his outstretched arms. He walked to the remains of the fire, now nothing but a small tendril of smoke crawling from the blanket of snow. He knocked the snow from the sticks of firewood, lay them on the wet coals and poked around for some hot coals that might still kindle a fire. Finding a small pile of black coals hiding some glowing ones, he knelt and blew on the smoldering coals and tinder and soon had flame. He sat back, looked around at the others, now stirring from their robes, and went to the pack to get the makings for coffee and sliced some meat to cook. He stuffed the coffee pot with snow, sat it at the side of the fire and skewered the meat on some willow branches and suspended them over the fire. He was joined by Joseph who offered help, but it wasn't needed. The others soon joined them and without speaking, took a share of the meat and began eating. With only two cups, Tatum and Joseph downed their coffee, poured more and offered it to the others, who gladly accepted and eagerly drank the hot brew.

Tatum sat across from Raven and asked, "What do you think our chances are?"

Raven looked at Longbow and said, "I think they are at their village already. If so, I do not think we can get the women back. There will be too many warriors and the women will be held as captives and guarded. It would take more warriors than we have."

"Well, I'm not ready to give up until I see where they are and know more," declared Tatum.

Raven looked at the man and remembered, "You came into our village alone, and you helped our people. That is the only reason you left alive. But if you try to enter the village of the Apache, they will kill you before you can even speak. They are fierce warriors and live only to kill their enemies. Even their name means enemy."

"My father taught me to never give up. He said if you can see the problem, you can find a solution and when you find the solution, get busy and solve the problem. So, I'll need to see the problem before I can find a solution," he stated emphatically, tossing a stick into the fire.

Raven looked at this man that had helped his people and had become his friend, wondered whether he was foolish or brave, and said, "We will go with you until we find the village. But then . . . " and he left the thought hanging between them. Both men knew the odds were against them with the weather and the Apache to contend with, but Tatum also knew he had no quit in him and was determined to do everything he possibly could to rescue both White Feather and Lizzie. He owed it to both of the women, White Feather as a friend that helped him to heal after the cougar attack, and Lizzie as she had trusted Tatum and counted him a friend. As his father had repeatedly told him, *It's always right to do the right thing.*

CHAPTER TWENTY
CAPTIVE

LIZZIE LAY ON HER SIDE IN THE DARKNESS. HER HANDS AND FEET WERE tightly bound, and she found no comfort on a thin blanket. The smells of the wickiup were a mix of smoke, cooked meat, and the musky smell of bodies. Crazy Wolf lay with his first wife under a heavy buffalo robe, his second wife lay near the two children, a boy of about nine or ten and a girl of five or six. When they arrived earlier that night, the two women scowled, spat, and beat Lizzie with sticks and rawhide thongs. Yet, Lizzie had detected an attitude of fear or distrust among the women and whenever they struck her, they would quickly jump back as if she could retaliate. Something was making the women wary of her, but she did not understand what. But she was bound and could not even move her hands, much less strike back. But there was something there she didn't understand but kept it in her mind.

The last time she ate was the snatched meat taken by White Feather and her stomach growled with hunger. She listened to the sounds of the camp, which were few, just an occasional scratching dog and a snort of a tethered horse. From beyond the camp, she heard the high-pitched tweets of a nighthawk and the repeated chirps of a yellow warbler. She tried to sleep, but her fear of the coming days made her more restless than her tired body could stand. The sudden cry of a coyote startled her and she waited for an answering cry from another. When it came she smiled as she remembered her Pap saying it was the cry of romance where the male calls to the female and is answered back. But the thought of her Pap and Momma brought a tear to her eye, and she thought of Joseph and wondered if he and Tatum would try to rescue them. She wanted to go back to the cabin and the peace she knew there, and as she thought of Joseph, she feared he would try to rescue her. Yet she knew the possibility of rescue from the midst of this village of more than twenty lodges would be beyond hope. She tried to roll to her other side, but could not and her movements brought the little girl to her side The child motioned her to be quiet and scowled to warn her of the danger of waking her father, Crazy Wolf. Lizzie nodded her head as best she could and lay back to be still, watching the little girl return to her blankets. *Well, maybe I have one friend,* thought Lizzie, forcing a slight smile.

Before first light, she was awakened by someone pulling at her bound hands. In the dim light of the still glowing coals she recognized the second wife, and Lizzie yielded to the woman's tugging to lift her to her feet. The wife put a finger to her lips, demanding silence, then reached down to unbind Lizzie's ankles, stood and motioned for Lizzie to follow. The two women slipped from the wickiup, pushing the entry blanket aside, and stepped into the cool of the morning. Lizzie was surprised to see the fresh snow that blanketed the village and gave a peaceful appearance to the cluster of wickiups and the few tipis. The sudden slap at her shoulder from the second wife caught her attention as the woman motioned for her to follow. The women walked to the trees with the dim light of pre-dawn making the snow sparkle in the moonlight, Lizzie recognized the beauty amidst the suffering and fear, and followed the woman. They gathered firewood, breaking dead branches from a couple of gnarled cedar and a few pinyon . Any loose firewood had been taken long before and the area was beginning to show the long stay of the Apache village.

When they returned, both with arms full of wood, they dropped the wood by the fire circle and the wife began stirring the coals, searching for any hot coals that would start their fire. Unsuccessful in her attempts, she motioned for Lizzie to follow and bring a couple of the pieces of wood. They went to a nearby larger fire circle that sat amidst a ring of wickiups, the woman stirred among the coals, grinned and used two sticks to pick up some coals and with Lizzie holding a wide flat piece of cedar. The woman placed the coals on the cedar and motioned for Lizzie to follow her back to their fire ring.

While Lizzie stood with the cedar and coals, the woman motioned for her to blow on the coals to keep them alive, while she brushed the snow from their fire ring and she made a cone shaped stack of firewood with some tinder and kindling at the center. When she was satisfied, she motioned for Lizzie to bring the live coals, and the woman, using a couple of sticks, took the coals and placed them at the center of the stack knelt before it and began blowing on the coals. Within moments flame licked at the kindling, caught and soon a fire was going. Lizzie stepped closer and held her hands to the flame for warmth, the woman joined her and smiled as the two stood side-by-side enjoying the crackling fire.

Lizzie was surprised when the woman spoke, saying, "I am Red Fox, you are Little Buffalo."

"Oh, yes, you can speak, I mean, you speak our language!" said Lizzie, excitedly.

Red Fox motioned for her to be quiet, "Wolf's first wife is Little Flower, she is pretty, but she is also mean. She was mean to me when I was brought here, and she does not like other women with Wolf."

"Yeah, when you hit me wid' dem straps, it hurt. But she hit me real hard, mebbe drew blood," said Lizzie, motioning to her back with her head. Her hands were still bound, and she lifted them toward Fox, but the woman shook her head and said, "I cannot. You must be tied."

"The children, dey yours?" asked Lizzie.

"No, I have only been here for two summers, I was taken from the Comanche."

Lizzie's eye grew wide as she asked, "Comanche? White Feather, the woman wid me, she is Comanche!"

Fox stepped back, eyes and mouth wide, and said, "White Feather is here?"

"Ummhumm, we was taken together," said Lizzie, nodding her head, "We been libin' up in da' mountains, an' dem 'pache snuck up on us and took us."

"But White Feather, she is chief Buffalo Hump's daughter!"

"Well, I don't know 'bout dat, she was stayin' wid' Tate Saint and helpin' us get ready for winter," explained Lizzie, confused.

Red Fox scowled, she couldn't understand why the daughter of the chief would be living with a white man and this dark girl. "Tate Saint, a white man?"

"Sho' is, an' a good one too."

"Will he come after White Feather," and added, "and you?"

"Dunno, he an' muh' brudda might, but, I dunno what they can do wit' so many."

"If they come and get you, will you take me too?" asked Red Fox, hopefully.

"Sho' nuff', that man ain't the kind to leave anybuddy behin'!" declared Lizzie, smiling.

As an afterthought, Lizzie asked, "Could you tell White Feather I be O.K.? And mebbe tell her to watch for Tate and Joseph?"

"Joseph is your brother?" asked Red Fox.

"Yeah, best brudder a girl could have," she stated, remembering the times together with her brother, "but could you tell White Feather?"

"I will try, but I heard Crazy Wolf tell Little Flower he gave her to our chief, Bear Killer. It will be hard, but I will try."

Their conversation was interrupted by Little Flower as she came from the wickiup, carrying a parfleche and a hind quarter of one of the deer brought in by the hunting party. She scowled at the two women at the fire and began barking orders to Red Fox, motioning to Lizzie, and Fox told her, "You hold the meat while I slice it!" And the day began for the captive Lizzie, wondering if she would ever know the freedom she long hoped for but found so elusive.

CHAPTER TWENTY-ONE
SNOW

WHITE FEATHER DUCKED WHEN THE OLD WOMAN TRIED TO HIT HER with a stick, chattering in Apache, thinking the captive could not understand. Another woman held a quirt of rawhide that she held high, ready to whip the addition to their lodge. White Feather's hands were bound together, but her feet were free and when the old woman struck at her, she ducked and grabbed the stick from her hands and threatened to strike her back, shouting, "No, my father is Buffalo Hump of the Comanche, and I am a Comanche warrior! You will not beat me!" She was grabbed from behind with an arm over her shoulder and a knife held at her throat.

The warrior that held her snarled into her ear, "Drop the stick before I paint it with your blood!" Feather complied, mumbling a threat to the women. She was spun around to face Spotted Pony, one of the hunting party, and was told, "You will do as my mother says, if you do not, your scalp shall hang in my lodge!"

The old woman, with a face of wrinkles that reminded White Feather of a rotten potato, and one eye that stared unmoving at the sky picked up the stick and waved it at Feather, directing her into the large buffalo hide tipi that was the lodge of the chief of this band of Apache. White Feather looked back at Spotted Pony, holding his knife before him, and bent to move the entry flap aside. As she entered, she heard the other woman address the older one as Crooked Eye, and Feather chuckled to herself at the appropriate name. She soon learned that Crooked Eye was the first wife of Bear Killer and the second wife, although not much younger and with no less intimidating appearance, was called Stone Woman. She knew the Apache family structure was dominated by the women, but the chief of the band was allowed as many as four wives, while the lesser chiefs, war chief and others, were only allowed two wives, but there was no limit to the number of captives that could be a part of the lodge. When Feather looked at the two old women, both with thinning white hair, she knew most of the work for this lodge would be put upon her, but she was determined to maintain her status as the daughter of a chief and a warrior, even if it meant she would have to fight for it.

She sat sullenly against the back wall of the tipi and watched as Crooked Eye talked to Bear Killer. This was the first time Feather would see the chief, and she tried to watch surreptitiously as the women spoke to him. Crooked became rather animated and the snatches of the conversation that Feather could make out were about taking the stick from her and threatening her, but Stone Woman broke in and added that Feather had said she was the daughter of the chief of the Comanche. This last comment brought a look of alarm to the face of the old chief and he looked at Feather and back at his wives. They continued their talk in muted tones, occasionally glancing in Feather's direction. She tried to appear disinterested and aloof, wanting to give them the impression she was not afraid of them. With no further demands made of her, White Feather sought to make herself a comfortable bed with the allowed blankets, and stretched out to sleep but was interrupted when the two women placed rawhide bonds on her ankles and left a long tether that Stone Woman wrapped around her own hand, scowling at Feather as a warning.

It was well before first light when White Feather was rudely awakened by a sharp tug on the ankle strap. The dim light of the night's fire showed Stone Woman standing by the entry way with a taut rawhide strap and motioning for White Feather to follow. She crawled from under the blankets, struggled to rise to her feet and hobbled her way to the entry and followed Stone Woman into the grey light of early morning. Crooked Eye snatched the second tether from the ground and snarled at White Feather, "You get wood, you go where we say, do as we say!" White Feather looked at the two women and saw their tactic was to trip her at any indication of disobedience.

With her wrists still bound tight, she started toward the trees near the riverbank. Her first stop garnered three large sticks, but she could only hold one while picking up the second, so she held her hands out to the women to undo the rawhide bonds. They looked at each other and at the captive, then Stone Woman slipped a knife from her waistband and stepped behind White Feather while Crooked Eye stepped in front of her to loosen the bonds. White Feather did not resist, and with the bonds loosened, she slipped her wrists from them but was stopped when Crooked Eye spoke, "No!" and wrapped the thong around one wrist and then the other, leaving a singular thong of about a foot in length, between her wrists, enabling her to pick up the wood but restricting her movement. She nodded her head at the woman and returned to the task of gathering wood.

After a short while, she had one arm full and was dragging a larger length of a limb as they walked back to the wickiup. When she dropped her arm load, Stone Woman suddenly jerked on the ankle tether, causing White Feather to fall, eliciting the laughter of the women. As she struggled to get up, Stone Woman jerked the tether again, pulling Feather's leg from under her, but Feather caught her balance and remained standing, but the lesson of never trusting was learned.

Snow had been falling since the middle of the night, but was only about three or four inches deep, but the cold and the snow were enough to make White Feather very uncomfortable without warm clothes or a blanket. She stood beside the fire trying to soak up some heat but was jerked to the ground again by Stone Woman. While Crooked Eye was busy preparing the meal, Stone Woman's task was to watch the captive, but one old woman was not enough to keep White Feather in check and she jerked against the tether and almost dumped Stone Woman in the snow. The old woman started shouting and Bear Killer stepped from the tipi, grabbed White Feather by the hair and jerked her back against him. Although an old man with stringy grey hair and more than his share of wrinkles and scars, he was still a strong warrior and White Feather could not resist his grip.

"So, Buffalo Hump's daughter is like her father, eh? Always fighting!" he growled into her ear as he held the flat of her back against his chest. He wrapped an arm around her waist and said, "If I were younger I would teach you what a real warrior could do, but since you are the daughter of a chief, I will let you be, for now." He pushed her away suddenly, and she stumbled to her hands and knees, but the threat was understood.

She looked back at the chief and snarled, "My father will kill all of you! Your village will be nothing but ashes!"

"But your father does not know where you are, and if he finds out, we will be gone before he can come," declared the chief. At his words, the two women, Crooked Eye and Stone Woman looked at their man in surprise. He ignored them and returned to the lodge, muttering to himself something about women.

Mid-morning saw White Feather dutifully scraping the hide of one of the deer brought in by the hunting party. The chief had his pick of the bounty and the hide had to be scraped of flesh and tallow. She was on her hands and knees as she stretched across the hide with the sharpened bone scraper and was startled by the appearance of a young woman leading Lizzie with a thong around her neck. Lizzie's hands were tied, and the woman spoke to the wives of Bear Killer in an angry tone, motioning toward Lizzie. She said, "I need your captive to instruct this dark woman in our way. She is stupid," and she tapped her head for emphasis, "and does not understand! Do you speak the white man's tongue?" she asked of Stone Woman who sat on a log, holding the ankle tether of White Feather.

"No!" spat Stone Woman.

"That one does!" declared Red Fox, motioning to White Feather, "I will use her."

Red Fox spoke to White Feather in Apache with venom in her words, "Tell this one to obey, or she will be killed!"

White Feather sat back on her haunches, looking at Red Fox curiously, and started speaking to Lizzie in the white man's language. "Lizzie, are you alright?"

"Yes, but I will act bad, she," motioning to Red Fox, "understands. She is like you, Comanche, and she knows you. She brought me here to see you."

White Feather looked from Red Fox to Lizzie and at Stone Woman. In Apache she asked Red Fox, "Does she not know what to do?"

"No, she is stupid!" answered Red Fox, motioning to Lizzie again.

"She said she is afraid, but she will learn if you are patient," answered White Feather, using words for the benefit of Stone Woman, who watched them carefully.

"I will beat her with the straps! Then she will learn!" declared Red Fox.

White Feather spoke to Lizzie, trying to sound as if she was warning her of Red Fox, but said, "our friends will come, be ready and watch for them."

Lizzie turned away from Stone Woman and grinned at the words of White Feather, nodding her head as she looked to Red Fox, the young wife of Crazy Wolf. She was startled when Fox jerked at the tether and started back to their wickiup. When out of earshot of the others, she listened as Red Fox said, "It was good to see White Feather, and I think she is right. Her people will come because she is the daughter of Buffalo Hump."

"Well, I think Tate and Joseph will come anyway. I jus' hopes they don't get themselves killed on account o' me and White Feather."

"We must be careful but watchful," stated Red Fox, hopefully, as she led Lizzie back to their wickiup and the work that awaited.

CHAPTER TWENTY-TWO
DISCOVERY

THE SNOW LET UP ABOUT MID-MORNING MAKING THEIR TRAVEL EASIER, but the wind began to cause a horizontal snowstorm. The men took shelter in a tree lined coulee that led into the Trinchera creek bottom. The windbreak was a welcome respite as they tethered their horses in the thick trees and they huddled against the stone walled bank. Joseph drug the parfleche with the smoked meat to their refuge and the men silently partook of the sparse meal. . Within the hour, the wind slowed, and the sun parted the clouds, showing blue sky over the creek. Tatum climbed the bank for a survey of the area just in time to see Dark Wolf return from his scout. At Tatum's signal, the man joined the group to give his report.

"Their village is below the lone mesa beyond the Conejos river, a big bend protects on three sides and the mesa behind. Four hands of lodges, been long time there," said Dark Wolf soberly. Four hands or twenty lodges told of at least thirty and probably as many as fifty warriors.

Raven looked at Tatum and motioned him closer as he bent to the sandy bottom of the coulee. Taking a stick, he began to draw what Dark Wolf had reported.

"This is the mesa," pointing at an oblong circle in the sand, "here is the river," pointing at a squiggly line away from the mesa, "and here is the village. We must cross the Rio Grande and then to the Conejos." Raven looked at Tatum to ensure his understanding, and continued, "They have four hands of lodges, too many for us to take. I will send Big Belly and Dark Wolf to our people for our father to know about the taking of his daughter, White Feather."

"How long for them to get there and back?" asked Tatum.

"Three, four days," answered Raven, "but, I do not know if they will come."

"Can we circle around behind this mesa and see the village?" asked Tatum, pointing at the sand drawing.

Raven looked at Dark Wolf for an answer, Wolf slowly nodded his head, and Raven said, "Yes, we can, but there are still too many Apache."

Tatum said, "You know, White Feather was telling me about some of the superstitions," and he noticed the scowl on Raven's face and explained, "uh, beliefs, of the Apache. I been thinkin' 'bout some of that and maybe we can use Joseph there to put some fear into 'em, whatchu think?"

Raven looked at the brawny black man and back at Longbow and let a slow grin cross his face and he nodded his head.

"Now, that ain't enough of a plan to free the women, but maybe it's a start. So, how 'bout you sendin' Dark Wolf and Big Belly on their way and we can start for the mesa and maybe come up with somethin' else?"

Raven turned to the two warriors chosen to report back to the Comanche village and gave them instructions and the men quickly mounted and rode away at a ground eating lope. Tatum looked at the clearing sky and uttered a quick prayer, *Lord, keep the weather away and let those two make good time. Oh, and it would also help to get us to the top of that mesa without getting spotted by the Apache.*

It was easy for the four, Tatum, Joseph, Tall Elk, and Raven, to follow the west bank of the Rio Grande. The crossing was easily done, and the bottom land of the Rio Grande held ample cover of cottonwood, alder, and oak brush. They were well away from the site of the village and they kept to cover, always watching the landmarks of the Sierra del Ojito and the larger Flat Top mesa to the South of the chosen mesa. When Raven judged them far enough south of the village, he motioned for the small group to turn to the west and make for the back side of the mesa.

A short while later the green of the valley fell away and they began traversing an alkali flat as they made their way westward. With only scattered clumps of sage and a variety of cactus for vegetation, every step of the horses kicked up the white dust of the dry alkali, choking both horse and rider. Soon the alkali gave way to the basaltic sand and adobe flats that led behind the mesa. Once past the first talus slope, a wide draw gave access to the top, cutting through the basalt rimrock and offering a steep climb to the mesa top.

As they crested the flat top mesa, the sun was dropping behind the distant stack of foothills and more distant San Juan mountains. The hazy light showed the different hills and mountains like shadows marching toward the sun. The lazy sun busied itself with painting the few remaining clouds with assorted shades of gold and orange. The men stopped and gazed at the Creator's beauty, enjoying the magnificent vista made all the more impressive by the lofty height of the mesa top.

Raven broke his stare to examine for cover and shelter. He motioned to the north edge where an upthrust of basalt provided a wall of protection. As they reined up before the wall, Tatum dropped to the ground and dug in his saddle bags for the spy glass of his father. He walked to a cut in the wall and peered over the edge at the wide valley below. Raven pointed at a wide flat shoulder of the mesa that extended like a woman's apron toward the winding Conejos river. He said, "In the shadow of that mound is a spring that flows toward the edge of the Apache village, there."

Tatum looked where Raven pointed, and at the end of the mound, the dwindling daylight made the cookfires of the Apache village appear like the lightning bugs Tatum remembered from his youth in

Missouri. He put the spyglass to his eye and scanned the distant village, seeing the many wickiups and the few tipis and the people moving about like tiny bugs in the distance. He looked at Raven and said, "We'll see more in the daylight, but we're well protected here. We can have a fire without it being seen."

Raven's attention was captured by the instrument in the hands of his friend and asked, "What is that?"

Tatum said, "Oh, here, put this to your eye and the other end toward the village. Like this," as he demonstrated. He handed it to Raven who copied the action of his friend, but when he saw the image, he dropped the spyglass down, and looked at Tatum and back at the glass, and said, "How?"

"Well, I don't rightly know, it has to do with this," he pointed at the glass in the end of the brass tube, "it just makes it bigger."

"Aiiieee, it is strange," said Raven, suspiciously.

Tatum chuckled and added, "We'll look again in the daylight and then make our plan. How 'bout we get somethin' to eat?"

"Yes, eat," responded Raven, still looking at the spyglass as he walked back to the beginnings of their camp.

MORNING BROUGHT a clear day with a warm sun that shed welcome warmth. Tatum returned to the cut in the wall to better survey the village and the flats below. Taking a comfortable perch, he lifted the spyglass and began scanning the village. He extended the length of the tube, bringing a clearer picture. Now he was able to make out the figures, recognizing the men and women and playing children. Centered in the village was a sizable tipi with wickiups arranged in a semi-circle before it. Tatum deduced this to be the lodge of the chief and watched the clearing before as the usual activity of the day began. He noticed a group of women, two that appeared smaller and a little stooped, and one that was taller and always between the other two.

He watched for a while until Raven joined him. Tatum described to him what he had seen and handed the spyglass to Raven to view the village. After a few moments of adjusting and manipulating, Raven finally was able to use the spyglass to survey the village. After a few moments, he lowered the glass and began to speak, "The tipi in the middle is the lodge of the chief. The women, the two smaller and stooped ones are his wives, but I think the center one, is White Feather. The way she moves tells me it is her."

Tatum took the spyglass and looked again, focusing on the women and spoke as he looked, "Yeah, I think you're right. That is White Feather."

Joseph had joined the men while Tatum's attention was centered on the village and as Tatum spoke, Joseph asked, "Can you see muh' sister?"

Tatum turned to look at Joseph, and answered, "I haven't yet. But if White Feather is there, I'm sure Lizzie is too."

Raven said, "Captives are separated, go to different lodges. White Feather was given to the chief, so your sister will be in another lodge."

"Is that good or bad?" asked Joseph.

"Not bad, but not good. Still captive. Different warrior has her, maybe war chief that led the raid or hunting party," explained Raven.

"So, what are we gonna be doin' to get 'em back?" asked Joseph.

"Well, we're thinkin' you're gonna have a lot to do with that," started Tatum, "you see, Joseph, Apache believe their bad spirits are all black, so you might become one of their bad spirits."

"And how do I become a bad spirit?" asked Joseph, tenuously.

Tatum began explaining what he knew about the Gans, or the spirits feared by the Apache, with Raven adding details and descriptions. Tatum pointed out the mound that extended toward the village and explained the plan that was just beginning to take form in his mind. He added, "Course we gotta get you down there and back up, leave no sign of your bein' there, and light you up at night. Now, soon's we figger that out, we'll take it from there. But that's just a little part of what we gotta do, cuz that won't be enough to get the women away. We still gotta work that part out."

"I thought we was gonna wait fer Raven's people to come, you know so we wouldn't be so outnumbered," stated Joseph as more of a question than a statement.

"Well, we don't rightly know if they're gonna come, and we sure don't know when," clarified Tatum. "So, we need to figger out somethin' just in case we gotta do it all by our own selves."

Joseph looked from Tatum to Raven, shook his head and walked back to the picketed horses. He busied himself with the horses, needing to move them often because of the sparse graze atop the mesa. He was not a thinker, his way was to just jump in and do what he could, but he knew it to be best to leave the planning and thinking to Tatum and Raven. He knew he still had a lot to learn about the wilderness and especially about the ways of the many Indians. He just hoped they would be able to get Lizzie back. After losing his Pap and Momma, he couldn't stand the thought of losing his sister. Somehow, someway, they had to get her back and he was willing to do whatever he could to make that happen.

CHAPTER TWENTY-THREE
PLANNING

HE WANTED TO KNOW ALL THERE WAS TO KNOW ABOUT THE APACHE village and the activities of the people. Tatum scanned the village with his spyglass most of the morning, with Raven and Joseph often relieving him, ensuring that nothing that happened in the village would go unseen. Joseph especially wanted to find Lizzie, but it was during Tatum's time at the glass when she was finally located. Tatum saw the girl exit a wickiup, following another woman, probably the wife of the warrior in the wickiup. Too far away to see anything more than enough to identify her, Tatum summoned Joseph to see what he believed to be Lizzie. When Joseph saw the figure he immediately exclaimed, "Tha's her, tha's Lizzie, sho' 'nuff! She be alive, glory! Thank you, Lawd, thank you!" He lowered the spyglass and looked to Tatum and asked, "How we gonna get 'em outta dere?"

"I've been thinkin' on that, Joseph," replied Tatum, "and I'm also thinkin' we need to do somethin' real soon. But let's go talk to Raven."

The two men climbed down from the perch atop the basalt wall and joined Raven by the fire. Raven quickly judged the approaching men had something to share and looked at Tatum when he said, "You have seen something?"

Tatum seated himself near the fire as he began, "Well, we spotted

Lizzie," and nodded toward Joseph, "his sister. But that's only part of it. I'm thinkin' they're 'bout to move the village. I've seen some of 'em stackin' stuff alongside their lodges, some have brought more horses into the village, and I'm thinkin' they're either movin' or some of 'em's headin' out on another hunt or somethin'.'"

"Ummm, Dark Wolf said the graze for the horses was almost gone, the woods look picked over for firewood, too much so for this to be their winter camp. If they move before Buffalo Hump comes, we will not get the women back."

"That's what I was thinkin', so mebbe we need to do somethin' to slow 'em up. Mebbe somethin' to keep 'em in their lodges or . . . "

Tatum began to explain the skeleton of his plan. It would require all of them acting together and they would have to start their preparations immediately. He began by drawing in the sand near the fire, showing the locations and the intended actions. Raven suggested a few changes, which Tatum readily agreed to and soon the men began to implement the plan.

————

Lizzie followed Red Fox from the wickiup into the bright sun of mid-day. They had finished smoking the meat on the racks alongside the cookfire and stored it in one of the parfleches in the wickiup. Little Flower had demanded they go for more firewood and to also find more of the Indian potato or any other edible shoots or plants. The women started for the wooded riverbank, Red Fox leading and Lizzie following at the end of the tether around her neck. Her hands were bound, and she did her best to act the disgruntled and angry captive, without going too far and forcing Red Fox to discipline her with the rawhide quirt.

When well away from the village, the two women searched the riverbank and talked, but only after ensuring no one was within earshot. Lizzie pulled up some onions and said to Red Fox, "I feel muh brother is some'eres near. I used ta' could allus tell when he was 'roun, and I'm certain sure he's some'eres near. We needs to be watchful."

"You don't think he'll come into the village, do you?" asked Red Fox, concerned.

"No'm, he ain't stupid 'nuff to do 'dat, but he be wid' Tate, an' they be gonna do sumpin' to get us outta here, I know dat!"

"What will he do?" asked Red Fox, almost in a whisper and looking around to reassure herself they were not heard.

"Don't know, but we needs to be ready. Oh, mebbe you oughta be tellin' White Feather!"

"White Feather is a warrior and some thought she should be a shaman. She will know what to do," shared Red Fox.

The basket held at the hip of Red Fox was full of the last of the onions, potatoes, cattail roots and a good portion of raspberries. She spoke softly to Lizzie, nodding her head toward the village and some approaching women, telling her they should return to the lodge. As they started back through the trees, both Lizzie and Red Fox were surprised when the approaching women were Crooked Eye, Stone Woman and White Feather. Red Fox greeted the women in Apache, but as she walked past White Feather she said, "She thinks her brother is near," nodding toward Lizzie.

White Feather looked to Lizzie with wide eyes and said, "Be careful!" Lizzie grunted a low response, but smiled at White Feather in understanding.

The rest of the day passed quickly, and the dusk of the evening saw many cookfires in the village. White Feather was finishing the scraping of the second deer hide and started to stand when a shrill whistle pierced the air and screamed into the camp. A long black arrow thudded into the ground beside the cookfire in front of the chief's lodge and the two women busy at the fire, screamed as they jumped to their feet, shouting a warning of attack.

White Feather looked at the arrow and immediately recognized the fletching and the length of the arrow as one from Longbow. She grinned as she heard another whistle screaming overhead and saw another arrow impale the side of a nearby wickiup. She looked at the near arrow, saw a small carved willow whistle strapped to the shaft of the arrow with thin strips of rawhide. She stepped to the arrow, ignoring the panic of the people of the nearby wickiups, picked up the shaft and quickly removed the whistle. She turned toward the tipi just as Bear Killer stepped out, looking around and seeing the arrow in the hand of White Feather, motioned for her to bring it to him. She complied, attempting to look afraid, and asked, "It is black! Is it from a Gans?" referring to the black spirit that held great power and even speaking of him struck fear into every child and many adults.

Bear Killer looked at the arrow, stepped closer to the fire ring, all the while searching everywhere for any sign of attack and saw nothing but women hurrying to their lodges, grabbing children on the way. A few warriors stood before their wickiups, also searching the village and the sky for any other cause for alarm. Two warriors, Crazy Wolf and another, trotted toward Bear Killer, bows with arrows nocked, and looking all about for any indication of attack. As they neared, another arrow fell from the sky and impaled itself in the ground, almost at the feet of Bear Killer. The chief dropped to a crouching stance, reaching for his bow as Stone Woman held it out to him. White Feather had neither heard nor seen the woman come and was surprised that she stood with no one holding the ankle tethers.

Crazy Wolf looked at the arrow, saw the angle of the standing shaft, and looked back in the direction that it would have come from, but there was nothing to be seen. The village was situated between the trees along the river and the rising mesa behind. Looking in the direction where the arrow came from, there were few trees or any other kind of cover. Everyone looked, showing confusion, and another arrow came from high above and thudded not more than two feet from the last. The warrior with Crazy Wolf, pointed and shouted, "Aiiieeeee. It came from the sky! There is no one there!"

Each of the warriors stepped beside the hide lodge of Bear Killer, and looked at one another as the chief spoke, "Wolf, you and three warriors, go, find those that have sent those black arrows!"

Wolf and the other warrior looked at Bear Killer in alarm, as they had not seen the arrows were black. Wolf asked, "Black Arrows? Are they from the Gans?"

"Spirits do not use arrows! Now go!" he commanded.

Wolf, followed by the second warrior, trotted toward the wick-iups near his and motioned to a handful of other warriors to follow. The group split, with three warriors following Wolf and four other warriors going the opposite direction. They would circle the camp, checking for any other sign of attack from any direction, and meet at the stream that came from the spring, before going any further. Wolf hoped they would find the mystery archer before they had to pursue what might be the black Gans. He thought about the black girl captive and wondered if she had anything to do with this strange occurrence.

CHAPTER TWENTY-FOUR
CONFUSION

THEY RODE AT A FULL LOPE, BUT THE DWINDLING LIGHT OF DUSK MADE them slow to a trot as they searched the trees at the river's edge and those lying between the river and the village. Wolf motioned for two of his warriors to ride through the trees while he and the remaining man would follow the wide bend of the river as they rode the circuitous trail around the village. Within a short while, the two groups met up at the small stream fed by the spring. Wolf directed the warriors to fan out and search for any sign of the archer that launched the arrows at the camp. At a walk, with nocked arrows on their bows, the group of eight warriors straddled the small stream and moved toward the spring that came from the base of the long hump that stood out from the tall mesa.

Often leaning from their mounts to search the ground for prints, the warriors warily made their way from the village to the spring. Nothing had been seen, no enemy warrior, no prints, no sign that anyone other than the villagers had been in this area. As they reached the spring, Wolf dropped to the ground and searched near the pool of water and the immediate area for any sign of the archer, but was disappointed. He stomped back to his mount and instructed the warrior known as Many Coups to return to the village and send an arrow toward the spring. Many Coups was known as an exceptional bowman and put his horse to a canter as he returned. He slid the horse to a stop near the fire ring by the chief's tipi, stepped down and lifting the bow high, he sent an arrow towards the spring. There was just enough light left for the remaining warriors to see the flight of the arrow that fell well short of the spring. Wolf said, "Aiiieee, no one can send an arrow as far as that!" referring to the arrows that hit the clearing earlier.

"We will search on foot," declared Wolf as he motioned to the men to again spread out and walk slowly back to the village, diligently searching for any sign of an enemy. But they were again unsuccessful and when Wolf reported to Bear Killer, he said, "There is no sign, no tracks, nothing that tells of a man that shot those arrows."

Bear Killer noted Wolf's reference to 'a man' and knew he was thinking of the black spirit known as the Gans that had great power and could move without sound or trace. The many tales told of the working of the Gans ranged from good to evil, mostly evil or death. On special occasions of celebration, there was usually one appointed to paint himself black and enter the dances as the Gans, usually to the delight of the people but more often to bring a respectful fear of the spirits. But neither Bear Killer nor Crazy Wolf had seen a black Gans except for those portrayed in the dances, and the thought of a real Gans caused concern in the hearts of both men.

———

IT WAS GETTING difficult to make out the activity of the village from atop the rimrock mesa, but Tatum had seen enough to know the initial work of their plan was accomplishing what they wanted. He turned to Raven and said, "They're runnin' around like they're mighty afraid of somethin', that's for sure."

"The Apache are known for their belief in the spirits. We too believe, but we have more that are good than evil. Some are tricksters, like the coyote, but more are good," explained Raven. The men walked together back to the fire ring and sat down as they reached for some of the fresh slices of venison hanging over the fire. Tall Elk had taken a deer from the back side of the mesa just after first light and now the men were well supplied for a few days as they waited for the arrival of the Comanche under Buffalo Hump.

"When we do this next thing, we must leave no sign. It would be best if Tall Elk and I do this," declared Raven as the men devoured the bloody but tasty venison steaks.

"You're probably right, neither Joseph nor I can move through the trees or anywhere like the two of you can. I think it best that we wait till well into the night, don't you?" asked Tate.

"Yes. The moon is in its last time and will not show much light. There are few clouds, so all we have is the light of the stars, but that will be good," observed Raven as he looked heavenward.

With all the men being light sleepers and with the horses tethered nearby, there was no need for a night watch and all turned to their blankets for some rest. Well after midnight, Tate and Raven rolled from their blankets, and Raven nudged the shoulder of Tall Elk to rouse him too. A break in the rimrock of the mesa held the only possibility of descending from the north side of the mesa top to the valley below. The break was concealed from the village by a cutback of the rimrock before the long finger of the mesa stretched out to the West. Tatum walked to the cut with the two warriors and watched as they descended, slipping and sliding in the loose shale and sandy soil, until they reached the bottom. They were to follow the back side of the extended mound, around the point and to the river's edge near the village.

The quiet of the night was stirred by a low whispering breeze that carried the sounds of the descent, but only as muffled movement of sand. The night birds were silent, even the coyotes had muted their chorus, with the only sound being the chuckle of the waters from the distant river. Tatum returned to the promontory, not expecting to see anything in the village, but needing to watch anyway.

ALL WARRIORS WOULD COMMONLY HAVE a unique shout or scream when they were going into battle and would sound that war cry as they charged. But Raven did not want the Apache to think they were being attacked by a war party, but rather to think only of the black Gans, so he thought about what sound he could make that would hopefully strike fear into the hearts of the villagers. He and Tall Elk had talked about what they would do, and Raven waited while Tall Elk made his way to the opposite side of the camp.

With enough time allowed, Raven stepped forward away from the trees, cupped his hands to his mouth and began a long wailing scream that pierced the darkness and echoed back from the far bluff. He screamed again, and turned to disappear into the trees. His cry had no sooner dropped into the darkness than a caterwauling wail of a mountain lion lifted from the far side of the village. Tall Elk had perfected the call as a youth and often used it to scare others when he was a youngster, and occasionally when he was the jokester on with a hunting party. But now the wail, as realistic as it was, made the villagers believe a mountain lion was preying upon their village. The cry was so real, the horse herd at the back side of the village began nervously prancing about, . Tall Elk quickly left before anyone could see him, leaving behind two tracks, made with his hands and stones, of a mountain lion.

Both Tall Elk and Raven had wrapped their feet with cuts from the fresh deer kill, with the hair out and loosely fit, so that any tracks left would be indistinguishable and confusing. Tall Elk had crossed over the river and trotted back upstream around the wide bend before crossing back to meet Raven. The agreed upon signal of the nighthawk sounded and Tall Elk made his way to the side of his friend, and both men trotted back to the point of descent from the mesa, retracing their steps as they climbed to the top.

TATUM WAS at the promontory and looking below. The darkness was pierced by pinpoints of light from freshly lit cookfires and carried torches. People were moving about, some quickly, others from wickiup to wickiup. A few torches were carried into the trees and toward the riverbank. Tatum was chuckling at the confusion as Raven and Tall Elk came to his side. He looked at Raven and said, "I could hear that scream clear up here! And that cougar cry you gave Tall Elk, almost made me start lookin' for it . It weren't that long ago when one o' them almost did me in! If it weren't fer White Feather, I'd prob'ly be dead now."

Raven looked at his friend with a scowl on his face and said, "I did not know this, when did this cougar get you?"

Tatum pulled the shirt over his shoulder to show the barely healed scars and said, "Oh, couple weeks ago. Thot I was a goner, but Feather came an' got me. I'd already killed the cat but he darnn near killed me."

Raven looked at Tatum thoughtfully and turned to look at the scampering torches of the valley below, wondering if White Feather was one of the torchbearers. There was more to their plan, but this was all they would do this night. Hopefully, this would not scare the village into moving sooner, but Raven thought they would spend tomorrow searching for the cause of the sounds and the arrows. Most leaders would want to dispel any fears before they moved, and Raven thought Bear Killer would do the same.

CHAPTER TWENTY-FIVE
GANS

WHEN FIRST LIGHT SHOWED THE VILLAGE BELOW, TATUM ADJUSTED the spyglass as he scanned the many wickiups and tipis, for any unusual activity. He noticed there was less busyness but more smoke coming from the smoke holes of the lodges, which meant most were staying inside to do their morning cooking over the fires in their homes. He chuckled at the thought of these warriors that were feared by most were now cowering within the safety of their lodges. Raven came to his side and he shared the spyglass, explaining as he did, "I think we accomplished what we set out to do, most of 'em's stayin' inside today. Don't think they'll be travelin' on this day."

Raven grunted at Tatum's comments and continued to scan the village with the spyglass. He said, "They will mount a war party to search for sign from the screams of the dark. What they find will only confuse them more." He turned away from the ridge and suggested they eat and make their plans for the day.

Joseph waited behind them and asked, "Ya'll see any sign of Lizzie?" When Tatum shook his head, Joseph asked to use the glass so he could look, and Tatum willingly complied.

Tatum had used the dim light of pre-dawn to set the stage for their next action by stacking some rocks,wood and green branches just below the rimrock cliffs directly below the escarpment where they spied on the village. Raven had explained about the legend of the Gans and how it told of his appearing before the face of a cliff to start his rampage. They wanted to invoke that legend and more. Raven and Tatum discussed their plans as they ate and shared the morning's coffee. Their plan called for nothing more until after dusk and with the busy night before, the men wanted to get some rest in before another hectic night.

Joseph busied himself with surveillance of the village, hoping for some sight of his sister, anything to assure him she was alright. He watched as she came from the wickiup and together with the other woman walked into the woods. Raven came to his side and said, "Mark the wickiup where your sister is, we must know where she sleeps. There is something we must do." Joseph knew of their plan, but he was so focused on what he must do, he did not know what else the plan entailed. Now that Raven spoke of his sister, Joseph became hopeful something would be done to rescue her.

After mid-day, Tatum relieved Joseph of his duties and with glass in hand, scanned the village. There was nothing unusual, but it appeared the normal activity had resumed, indicating the village had overcome some of the confusion and fright. He looked at the sky, noted there were only a few clouds hanging over the Western mountains, but overall a clear blue sky with plenty of sunshine. He had listened to Carson speak of what he called Indian Summer as a time after the first chill or even first snow of the winter, there was a time of a few weeks when the weather was almost like summer with blue skies and warm temperatures. *Maybe that's what we've got now, Indian summer. Humm, I kinda like it. Maybe after this, I'll have more time to work on the cabin and stuff.*

As he pondered the warm day and the activity of the village, he frowned as it seemed the light was growing a little dim. He looked around, back at the sky and saw no clouds, but felt a little drop in temperature and considered the dim light, wondering if there was something wrong with his eyesight. Shielding his eyes, he looked toward the sun, criss-crossed his hands showing a pin-hole between the fingers and looked closer still at the sun. He suddenly realized what he was seeing, and turned to Raven and motioned him over.

"Quick! We need ta' get Joseph set and down there. He needs to start his dance!"

"Before dark? Why?" asked a surprised Raven.

"No time to explain, but I think there's a eclipse comin' and it'll work in our favor. Hurry! Get Joseph!"

Within seconds, Joseph was at the side of Tatum and Raven as they prepared what would be his costume. Tatum reached for some ashes, smeared them around Joseph's eyes, making him look like a ghostly figure. Raven fitted a black flat angular headdress on him as he pulled on a dark breechcloth. Joseph stood and looked questioningly at Raven and Tatum, saw their slow growing grins and knew he was ready.

Tall Elk had already lowered himself below the escarpment and was preparing a fire, hidden from view of the village, for their use. With Tatum's ropes, the men lowered Joseph to the prepared site. He crouched below the rocks while Tall Elk fanned the flames of the group of small fires. Joseph looked at the sky, noticing the dimming light and cooler temperatures, shook his head in wonder, craned to look up at Tatum, but he could not be seen. Tall Elk looked to Joseph, and when he nodded his head, Elk used the green branches to make the fires smoke. Joseph stood, head dress on, and holding a lance over his head, he screamed as loud as he could and began dancing in the smoke, shouting in an angry jibberish. Tatum had instructed him to point at the sun often, shouting as he did, and Joseph used his deep voice, amplified by the cliff face behind him, and shouted the warnings to the village below.

Although they knew that whatever was said by Joseph might not be heard below, Raven had given him a smattering of words in Apache for him to use. He chanted, *Deeyá łizhįį ch'eekéé deevá isdzáníí* and paused, pointed upward and said simply *Ya'íí.* He was told that would say *Leave black girl, leave woman. Sun!* He enthusiastically and loudly repeated the Apache words, hoping they could be heard and would be obeyed.

Although only a partial eclipse, it was enough of a darkening of the usually bright afternoon sun to frighten the people. And with the sudden appearance of the legendary spirit Gans, the people were almost in a panic, not knowing whether to go into their wickiups, flee to the woods, or simply run away. The steadfast women won over and grabbed their children as they ducked into the lodges. Warriors tried to show their bravery with some shaking shields and lances at the Gan, but the darkening sun tipped the scales of judgment in favor of hiding in the lodges.

Within a short time, the village appeared empty, and Tatum and Raven dropped the ropes over the embankment to lift Tall Elk and Joseph back to the top. The remaining smoke from the fires obscured their timely escape and all were soon ensconced behind the wall. Tatum was chuckling at the response of the people, but Raven and Tall Elk looked at the white man with wonder. Raven asked, "How did you know about the sun?"

Tatum forced himself to stop laughing as he began to explain, drawing in the sand for better understanding, and said, "It's what is called an eclipse. When the moon hides the sun. You know, as the moon passes over during the night and sometimes is still seen during the day, well, every once in a while, it passes between us and the sun." He held his hands up to demonstrate, "And when it does, it's called an eclipse. I read about it in the Boston newspaper when it happened a few years back. They said it would happen again in a few years, so, guess it did!"

Raven and Tall Elk looked at the white man with wonder and skepticism in their eyes, shook their heads and started to turn away when Joseph said, "I 'member that. That was when Nat Turner thot it 'twas a sign and started the uprisin' of slaves that got us kicked outta our homes. That was when Pap and us were bought by Mr. Thomas. Yeah, I 'member."

Tate looked at Joseph and nodded his head, still chuckling at what had happened. He called to Raven and said, "We still gonna do that down yonder?"

Raven looked at Tatum and nodded his head and added, "My father could be here soon, maybe when the sun rises again. Then we can attack these Apache and teach them the way of the Comanche," he spat.

Tatum looked again at the village, using his spyglass, and his muttered, "Oh Oh, trouble!" brought the attention of Raven, causing him to return to the overlook.

In front of the chief's tipi, a group of warriors had converged and were animated in their actions, pointing toward the mesa and chattering. Raven watched, took the spyglass and gazed at the group. He looked at Tatum and said, "They will come to see if this Gans is real. We cannot let them find the place where he stood."

"Well, let me see if I can stop that. Raven, take a couple more of my arrows and get 'em good an' black. Ya' got anymore o'them whistles?"

"No whistles," he answered as he used the coals to blacken the arrows.

Tatum grabbed his longbow and stepped near the cut in the wall, accepted the arrows from Raven and said, "You watch an' let me know where the first one lands."

Tatum stepped into the bow, extended his arm, drawing the string back with the other, bringing the arrow to its full length, and lifted the bow slightly and let the arrow fly. It sailed high and slowly began to lose its arch and began the drop toward the village. The arrow buried almost half its shaft into the ground less than five feet from the fire circle in the main clearing in front of the chief's tipi. The sudden thunking sound caused all of the clamoring warriors to turn and look at the arrow. They froze, but when another came dropping from out of the blue, the warriors scattered to find cover.

As the people peered from behind wickiups and tipis, none could see where the arrows came from, thinking only the Gans from high up on the mesa could have sent the arrows from such a distance. Mumbling and nervous chattering began to fill the village as the once brave warriors retreated to their lodges. Bear Killer returned to his tipi and stepped inside to the silence of the women. It was rare that one of the warriors would enter his tipi with the women present and find nothing but silence. The wives were not known for their reticence, but he was glad he didn't have to explain what he did not understand.

RAVEN LOOKED at Tatum and grinned as he said, "They have run to hide in their lodges."

Tatum chuckled and laid his bow aside as he stepped to the wall to look below. He turned to Raven and said, "So, you think Buffalo Hump might be here as soon as tonight?"

Raven nodded his head but added, "He could be here then, if he is coming, it will be no later than after the sun rises again."

It was just after dusk yielded to darkness when the actions of the afternoon were repeated. This time the chosen site was atop the mound nearer the village and well within the hearing of all in the village. They carefully prepared the site with a mound of rocks to hide the flames and the presence of Tall Elk, while Raven set off on another part of the plan. When Joseph was ready, the fire was fanned to life and he again screamed to the village. He began to dance and wave the lance as he shouted the words in Apache again and again. The flames flickered and cast long shadows that made his appearance even more intimidating, and at the chosen signal, both Tatum and Tall Elk snuffed out the flames, so they could make their escape. As planned, they quickly covered the trench that held the fire, moved the rocks on top, scattered loose dry dirt and sticks, drug blankets across their tracks and carefully utilized rocks and grass to make their escape, with their feet bound in deer skin.

As Joseph did his dance, Raven stealthily entered the village, went to the wickiup of Crazy Wolf and while the man and his women stood beside the wickiup mesmerized by the dancing Joseph, Raven placed a turquoise covered water pot beside Lizzie's blankets, and made his escape without notice.

CHAPTER TWENTY-SIX
RETURN

THE LEGEND OF THE BLACK GANS AMONG THE JICARILLA APACHE WAS one of crossing over to the other side when one dies bravely in battle. The role of the black Gans was to allow or prevent one from crossing over. The legend also told of the black Gans demanding his own sister be left behind and signified this by placing a turquoise water jug by her sleeping robes. The Inde , or people of the Jicarilla Apache, believed in the power of the black Gans, not so much as an evil spirit, but as one that could keep the soul of an Apache from crossing over to the other side, or the Apache belief in the hereafter.

Crazy Wolf was preoccupied with what he had just seen when the black Gans danced before the fires on the knoll nearer the village. He was angry with himself for feeling fear of this black being, but fear he felt. He stormed into the wickiup, throwing aside the entry flap and diving for his sleeping robes. A low fire simmered in the central pit and dim light filled the dark wickiup, but when the light flickered, something caught the eye of Wolf. He sat up with a sudden jerk, looked to the robes near the back of the lodge and saw something out of place. He stood and stretched for the item but recognized the turquoise water pot before he touched it and snatched his hand back as if burnt. He looked around the lodge nervously for anything else that was foreign and backed slowly to the entry, bumping into Little Flower as she tried to enter. He pushed her back, never taking his eyes off the pot in the shadowy wickiup, pushing the women away from the entry.

He dropped the entry flap, turned and snarled at Lizzie and barked, "She is one! The black Gans has spoken of her!" He backed away from the girl as if she was made of molten lead and could burn him. His eyes grew large and he dropped to a slight crouch, snarled at Red Fox to cut the rawhide thong and the bonds at Lizzie's wrists. He spoke to Little Flower, "Get that thing out of my lodge!" pointing to the wickiup.

Little Flower cautiously entered the wickiup and looked about in the dim light. When she spotted the turquoise water pot, she screamed, "Aiiieeeee" and backed out of the wickiup without touching the pot. When she came from the lodge empty handed, Wolf back-handed her, knocking her to the ground. He looked at Red Fox who was standing dumbfounded, and snarled at her, "Get that pot out of the lodge or I will kill you!" Red Fox stepped through the entryway, saw the pot at the far side and picked it up, grinning at the thought of whoever placed it here. She sobered her expression, trying to show fear, and walked from the lodge to see Wolf pointing toward the woods for her to take the pot from the village. "Bear Killer must know of this," declared Crazy Wolf as he turned, grabbed at Lizzie's tunic, caught the fringed sleeve and trotted toward the lodge of the chief, dragging the girl with him.

Wolf was surprised to find Bear Killer seated before the fire with others around the circle. These were the elders of the village and leaders of the Gulgahén, or Abáachi Mizaa. Usually Crazy Wolf, as a war leader, would be included in this council, but he had not been invited. When he approached the circle dragging the black girl, he interrupted the council with his report of the turquoise water pot left by the black girl's robes. This caused an immediate stir of comments and discussion, with alarm showing on most faces until Spotted Pony, the son of Bear Killer stood to speak. "What our brother tells us of this water pot is the same as the stories of black Gans making a demand to leave the young girl behind. But I question if this is done by the Gans or by someone trying to fool our people."

Wolf stepped forward, leaving Lizzie standing alone, and snarled, "Do you think I would try to fool our people? The pot was left in my lodge because of this woman! It was left there by the Gans!"

"Did you see it placed there?" asked Spotted Pony with a grin starting as he lowered his head to look at Wolf from under his thick brows.

"It was there when we turned away from the black Gans that danced on the knoll!" shouted Wolf, defensively.

"Ahhh, so our brother," started Spotted Pony as he looked around the circle, "did not see it put there. So, someone else, even this woman," motioning toward Lizzie, "could have put it there." Spotted Pony had been a rival of Crazy Wolf and coveted his position as war leader for many summers. Now he saw an opportunity to discredit and mock the man.

"Instead of fear, we should be angry! This could be a trick of the Comanche or the white man to make our people feel that which an Apache should never feel, fear!" He dropped into a slight crouch and pointed at the other members of the council as he continued, "Our brother has been so afraid of the black Gans he probably wet himself!" Several of the council members stifled a laugh as they watched the performance of Spotted Pony. "The stories of our grandfathers say the black Gans is not evil, but a guide for our people to the other world. If this is really the black Gans, then instead of fear, we should dance to celebrate that he has come to show the way! Let those that are so evil they cannot cross over and would be stopped by the Gans, show fear. We," pointing around the circle, "should celebrate someday crossing over."

Crazy Wolf had listened and watched as Spotted Pony sought to put him down, and when the man finally seated himself, Crazy Wolf began, "Our brother, Spotted Pony, does not believe the stories of our grandfathers, instead he mocks them! We have been taught to respect our grandfathers and the lessons they teach us, but Spotted Pony would have you to believe this is the work of some puny white man. There is no white man that could show himself as a black Gans! We have been warned, and those who do not heed this warning, our grandfathers have taught us the black Gans will prevent those from crossing over and will be doomed to wander in the darkness forever! I say we leave this place, and we leave this sister of the black Gans behind! This is what the legends say!"

Bear Killer rose to his feet, looked around the circle and began, "We have heard from two of our brothers. Both of these men are proven warriors and respected leaders of the Gulgahén. We," he motioned around the circle of the council, "must decide what our people are to do. If this black Gans is a true spirit, do we heed his warning? What if he is not real? Do we seek him out? If we are to seek him, who will go? Will any of our warriors want to go on a quest in search of what might be the spirit of our legends? These questions must be answered." He sat down as the others nodded their heads and looked to one another. It was up to the council to decide what must be done.

———

DARK WOLF WAITED at the campfire as Raven and Tatum arrived. Although a little surprised, Raven greeted Dark Wolf and asked, "Is my father coming?"

"Yes, they will be here before first light. I must go back to them to guide them here. Is White Feather and the other one still with the Apache?"

"Yes, but the Apache grow restless, we have done some things to scare them or even to anger them. We must move against them soon or they will be gone. Take that message to Buffalo Hump."

Dark Wolf looked from Raven to Tatum and stood to leave. He spoke to Raven, "I must change horses, my mount must rest." Raven motioned for him to take one of the tethered horses and turned back to the fire and looked at Tatum. "We must be ready. I think the Apache might leave at first light, we cannot let them take White Feather."

"I agree, but what do you think we should do?".

Joseph and Tall Elk had joined the group and heard the comments of Raven prompting Joseph to declare, "We ain't gonna leave Lizzie, neither!"

Tatum looked at Joseph and reassured his friend, "No, we ain't gonna let either of the women be taken. We've gone to too much to let them be taken now." He looked to Raven, waiting for his explanation.

Raven sat back and began to explain about the legend of the black Gans, the usual actions of the Apache and their nomadic ways before the winter set in. He explained what Buffalo Hump would probably want to do about any attack on the Jicarilla. Tatum and Joseph listened, nodding and commenting occasionally, as the four men developed a plan to hopefully ensure the rescue of the women. But most of their plan was dependent on the response and actions of Buffalo Hump.

CHAPTER TWENTY-SEVEN
ENCOUNTER

IT WAS NIGHTMARE BLACK WHEN WHITE FEATHER WAS KICKED awake. The old women were rustling about, gathering the parfleche and packs, taking them from the lodge. A small fire in the center of the clearing gave little light, and Feather knew the village was readying to leave. Stone Woman spoke in a harsh whisper, ordering her to carry the robes and packs from the tipi. She stood and reached for the robes, only to stumble on the long tether. She grunted and motioned to Stone Woman to remove the tether, so she could move freely. Stone Woman looked to Crooked Eye and the older woman cackled, "Do it!"

When Feather stepped out of the tipi, she looked skyward and saw the stars had retreated behind the darkness and she felt a moisture in the air. The dim light from the fire showed a fog had settled in and she feared it would hide the move of the village, making it difficult for her people to find them. Stone Woman hissed at her and Feather responded by going back into the tipi for more bundles. Within a short while, the tipi's lining was taken down by Stone Woman and Crooked Eye was busy with the pegs around the outside. Feather was given the task of removing the willow pins that held the covering together. Once the last pin was removed, the hide covering slid down the poles to be gathered and folded by the women. The lodgepoles were lowered and used to make travois for carrying the many bundles. Feather could tell by the whisper of movements; the entire village was preparing to move at first light.

They were heard before they were seen. The muffled thunder of galloping hooves brought everyone's attention to the rear of the camp. The usually quick responding warriors of the Apache were frozen in place as the ghostly apparition of the attackers pushed their way through the thick veil of fog. The Comanche warriors had crossed the alkali flats to reach their point of attack and the dusty white alkali had painted both man and beast to give them the appearance of the spirits of the dead. When the screams of their war cries broke the stillness of the morning, the death songs and cries of the Apache added to the din. What had been an orderly working of the people to prepare for their move, now became a pandemonium as they tried to flee with bundles and tipi poles.

Arrows whispered through the dim light and lances found purchase in the flesh of the few that stood to defend themselves and their village. Screams of women and children became sounding knells for the attackers to find their targets. The sudden onslaught caught the village completely by surprise and the Apache warriors floundered in their search for their weapons. The thuds of tomahawks splitting skulls were accompanied by the defiant war cries of those that launched arrows and lances at the attackers. Horses were downed by both lance and arrow and the riders were quickly dispatched, sometimes by women and youngsters. Most of those that died went to meet their Maker, certain they had been killed by a spirit. No one noticed the breaking of light through the fog, but the rays of sunlight gave direction to the few that escaped into the woods, but also made targets of those that had hidden behind the debris of the camp.

The remaining horse herd of the Apache had stampeded away into the woods only to be stopped by the river, but once a few jumped from the bank into the water, the rest followed. Most of the herd had been gathered by the wickiups and tipis to be loaded with travois and bundles, and the attack spooked many of them to run off with travois bouncing behind or bundles to be dragged away. White Feather had swung aboard the horse that was to be used for the travois for the tipi and lay low on its neck as she directed the animal toward the wickiup of Lizzie and Red Fox. As she approached the skeleton of the structure, she saw Lizzie tethered to the frame and Feather dropped to the ground to free her friend. Lizzie gave a grin of relief, but she began stammering, "They took Red Fox, we have to get her, I promised!"

The sounds of the attack had not diminished as the Comanche found some hidden or fleeing warriors and brought their wrath on their long-time enemies. Feather lifted Lizzie to her feet, swung aboard the horse and reached down to help her friend. She turned to tell her, "I must have weapons, we will get them from Bear Killer." She dug her heels into the ribs of the horse and wheeled it about to return to the site of the downed tipi. As they approached, she saw Raven standing astraddle of the body of Bear Killer, holding his scalp high and screaming his war cry.

"My brother has shown himself mighty to kill the chief Bear Killer! Even though he was an old man!"

Raven turned at the sound of White Feather's voice and grinned at his sister, "I thought they had taken you again!"

"Ha! His old women are still thanking the spirits I did not go with them!" she replied.

Tatum and Joseph slid their horses to a stop behind Raven. When Tatum saw White Feather it brought a smile to his face, but Joseph had not seen Lizzie and shouted, "Where's Lizzie?"

She leaned around White Feather and said, "Heah I is, brudder!" and slid to the ground to run to him. Joseph dropped to the side of his mount just in time to catch Lizzie and lift her off the ground with a bear hug as he shouted, "Glory be! Thank da Lawd!"

"And Buffalo Hump and his warriors," added Tatum, grinning at the reunion.

When Joseph let Lizzie stand, she pushed away from him and looking at Tatum and Raven said, "We gotta get Red Fox!"

Tatum said, "Who's Red Fox?"

Raven looked at White Feather and saw her nodding her head as she answered, "Red Fox is one of our people. Her father was a close friend of my father in his youth."

"I promised! I promised we would take her wid us!" pleaded Lizzie.

Buffalo Hump rode up to the side of Tatum, looking at his son and daughter with a wide grin on his face. He looked to Tatum and said, "We meet again my friend," as he extended his hand in greeting. The battle was all but over, with the only cries coming from the wounded or shouts of victory by some warrior gaining plunder. Buffalo Hump looked at his son and said, "We have done well, this was a good battle. We have killed many of our enemy and we have White Feather."

"Yes, but I am told another of our people is still held by those that ran away. She is the daughter of your friend; her name is Red Fox," explained Raven.

Buffalo Hump reacted like he had been struck, scowled at Raven and said, "Do you know this for certain?"

White Feather interjected, "I talked with her, she asked us to take her away from these Apache!"

"Our horses have traveled far, we cannot go. But you and these," pointing at Tatum and Joseph, "have fresh mounts. You can go! There are few warriors left, bring back the one called Red Fox!" ordered Buffalo Hump. He reined his mount around and signaled to his warriors, so they could prepare to leave.

White Feather looked at Raven and said, "I will go too."

Lizzie chimed in, "An you ain't leavin' me b'hind!"

CHAPTER TWENTY-EIGHT
CHASE

THE REMAINING BAND OF APACHE LED BY CRAZY WOLF WAS MOSTLY women and children. The only warriors were Wolf, Snake Eater, Quills-in-Nose, and Horse, but there were three young men, not yet proven warriors, that sought the honor. Before the attack, Wolf had been given the task of leading the village to their new camp by Bear Killer and had already started with a handful of the villagers. He knew his responsibility was to get those with him to safety and he drove them on to make their escape. There should have been more, but before the rest were ready to travel, the Comanche came to seek their vengeance.

This band of the Jicarilla were part of the people known as the Llaneros or Gulgahén, the Plains People of the Jicarilla. Their territory lay east of the Rio Grande and South to Taos Pueblo in New Mexico territory, but now they were moving west into the territory of the Olleros or Saidindê, the mountain dwellers of the Jicarilla Apache, who considered the Rio Grande to be the line between the two territories. Although both were Apache, they were not the same people. Also, the Llaneros had allied themselves with the Caputa Ute while the Olleros were allied with the Muache Ute. Two different bands of

Apache and two different bands of Ute with one unifying principle, all were enemies of the Comanche.

Now, Tatum and Joseph traveled with two Comanche into the heart of enemy territory to rescue one Comanche woman that wanted nothing more than freedom.

The trail of the fleeing Apache was easy to follow, shortly after leaving camp they crossed over the Conejos River and were following the river upstream, staying just outside the fringe of the willows and cottonwood. Tatum suggested they split up with some on either side of the river in case they crossed back over.

Raven said, "The band of Bear Killer are of the Llaneros and Crazy Wolf is leading his party into the land of the Olleros, or mountain dwellers. He may try to find their winter camp and join them or have them join him to come against the Comanche."

"Well, we best catch up to 'em 'fore they find their friends. I ain't in the mood to take on another whole village. One's 'nuff, don'tcha think?" asked Tatum.

Raven let a grin cut his face and he let a chuckle escape as he answered, "One village is enough!"

"Alright then, you take Joseph with you, an' me'n the women'll keep the pack mule. We'll stay 'tween the river an' the hills yonder, you two watch yourselves, there ain't much cover on that side."

Raven and Joseph followed the obvious trail, staying as close to cover as possible, but the Apache were moving fast and cared little about cover. Raven believed the pursued Apache would be certain the rest of the Jicarilla would easily stop the attack of the Comanche and would soon join them. Raven kept a vigilant watch before them, not wanting to make himself seen before he spotted the fleeing tribe. Joseph hung slightly back, deferring to the experience of the proven warrior and man of the wilderness.

Tatum led the small group staying well covered from the opposite bank of the shallow river. The stunted cottonwood, thick alder, abundance of willows and berry bushes, kept them from view of anyone across the water. He watched as the trail grew more narrow and he looked ahead to see a hillock that reminded him of an old sway-back plug horse that the neighbor Johnson had for his fields in Missouri. The tall mound had a razor ridge atop fractured basalt rock, a sway-back dip in the middle and bent around toward the larger mesas. With tapered sides that resembled the mounds of the red and black ants found in the plains, the hummock and its singular features stood out from the larger flat-topped mesas in the area. The river hugged the tapering shoulders, allowing a narrow trail of grass as the passageway moved around the knoll.

Mid-afternoon Raven and Joseph crossed back over the river to re-join Tatum and the others, as they chose to give the horses a brief rest and enjoy a respite for themselves.

"I think we are closing on them. They will stop at the joining of the rivers," stated Raven.

"Are we better off on this side or the other'n?" asked Tatum.

"This river moves away from the hills before the other joins it. We will cross a white flat before and then there will be a good place to find cover behind a long low mound," explained Raven. "The Apache will still be on the far side, but it is there they decide to go to the Llaneros country or turn back to the Pinyon Hills and beyond to their country."

They had been traveling south alongside the river and were at least three to four days travel from their cabin or from the Comanche village. They knew whatever they did would have to be done of their own accord, there would be no one coming to help. Any mistakes they made would be costly, even fatal, and Tatum did not want to risk the lives of the women again nor of his friends, but Lizzie had promised and there was a young woman that was hoping for rescue.

The lowering sun stretched the shadows over the five would-be rescuers. The alkali flat had been crossed and the silhouette of the finger like knoll before them stretched across their way extending back to the tree covered hills in the distance. The thick cottonwood and alder near the river invited them to stop while there was still some twilight to guide them.

Raven motioned he would go to the top of the mound and scout the location of the Apache camp. Tatum reached back into his saddle bag and offered the spyglass to a grinning Raven who gladly accepted. He still marveled at this magic of the white man that gave him sight of things so far away.

Tatum watched as Raven, now afoot, trotted to the long mound and started up the adobe soiled hillock. Tatum stepped down and joined the others as they tethered the mounts within reach of riverbank grass and dropped the packs from the mule and the saddle from his horse. They readied their camp but would not start a fire until Raven returned with word of the Apache camp.

As he approached the crest of the wide knoll, Raven dropped to hands and knees and slowly neared the top. Dropping to his belly, he looked to see another knoll that would have to be crossed before he could see beyond into the river bottom. He looked around at the lack of any cover, save scattered clumps of bunch grass, stunted sage, an abundance of prickly pear and cholla cactus. He started his belly crawl, slowly moving across the rough surface of adobe, sand and gravelly soil. Forced to take a winding route to avoid the cactus, it was several minutes before he neared the far shoulder of the knoll. The light was dim, but he could still see enough to make out shadows and the tree lined banks of the river. Using a weather-worn sandstone as cover and a rest for the spyglass, he began scanning the bottomland for sign of the Apache camp.

Tucked into a large cluster of cottonwood, was the sought for camp. They had fashioned some simple shelters with bent over saplings and branches, laid out their robes and blankets for bedrolls and were preparing their meals over small cook fires. As Raven looked, he slowly moved the glass along the riverbank searching for the horse herd or any warriors set on watch. the head and shoulders of an approaching Apache filled the lens of the glass and Raven jumped back, certain the warrior was upon him and about to strike. But when he dropped the glass, there was no one, and suddenly realizing what he had seen, he looked beyond the sandstone and saw a shadowy figure climbing the hill but at least thirty yards away. Raven dropped his head into the shadow of the stone, lay the spyglass aside and drew his tomahawk and knife, bringing his legs up beneath him, ready to pounce.

Snake Eater, one of the few warriors with Crazy Wolf, had been tasked with climbing the knoll and watching for the approach of the rest of the village. He was not expecting to see anything but did as he was told. With head down and mumbling to himself, he glanced up to see the wide smooth sandstone and thought it would be a good perch to watch over the camp. Within a few strides, he reached the stone, turned and sat down. He leaned forward to rest his elbows on his knees.

Just then Raven, slipped up behind Snake Eater, grabbed his hair and quickly drew his knife across his throat, letting only a short grunt escape from his quarry. Blood cascaded over the knife and hand of Raven as he pushed his knee into the back of the Apache and jerked back on the long, wrapped braids. Snake Eater slumped forward, kicking his legs out in a last spasmodic jerk, and Raven pulled on the hair, using his knife to free the scalp from the dead man.

Raven pulled the body from the sandstone promontory, dragging it back away from the shoulder of the knoll. He kicked dirt and gravel over not to bury it but to just make it more difficult to find in the darkness. He returned to the sandstone, retrieved the spyglass and looked again at the camp. Satisfied with what he had seen, he moved back from the shoulder, stood and trotted across the wide knoll and down to the camp of his friends. Now they must decide how best to get the girl from the camp before the Apache found their missing warrior.

"ALL I COULD SEE WAS THREE WARRIORS PLUS THE ONE I KILLED," SAID Raven as he shared his observations. He continued, "Three young ones, not yet warriors, were with the horses. The rest were women and children,"

"Ya think they'll be sendin' up one o' them warriors to switch off with the one ya killed?" asked Tatum.

"Not soon, but one will come."

"Hmmmm," pondered Tatum, resting his chin in his hand as he sat spread-legged with elbows on his knees, and chewing on some smoked meat. He sat back and looking at Raven started, "How 'bout we . . . nah," and dropped back on his elbows. "Ya say there's three of 'em left?"

"Yes, and the boys with the horses."

Joseph piped up with, "Wal, there's three of us, too!"

White Feather elbowed Lizzie and nodded at the girl, bent to whisper something just as Tatum said, "I know. Here's what I'm thinkin', now you tell me if I'm wrong about this . . . " as he scooted forward on his seat, and began detailing a plan, trying to describe everything with hand and arm motions, wishing he could draw in the dirt, but there was little light to see. After he finished as much as he could, Raven interjected, "Joseph should go to the mound for the warrior that will come for the dead man."

"You're right about that, an' if that man sees the black Gans, no tellin' what he'll do!"

The small group gathered closer together to discuss the details of the plan, knowing they were going against greater numbers than just the three warriors. The women of the village could and would fight for the men and for their own protection. They would have no way of knowing the attackers were just after one woman.

Joseph was the first to leave. The timing of the relief for the lookout was unknown and unpredictable and he had to be ready with the rest of the plan as well.

He disappeared into the darkness as the others prepared themselves. Leaving the animals tethered, they started into the starlit night together, crossed the shallow river, and prepared to stagger their approach. As they neared the camp, Raven swung wide into the flats, finding cover among the scrub brush and sage, while Tate started close in along the river bank. Lizzie was to wait, prepared to fetch the animals or whatever would be needed. She was armed with her bow and a full quiver of arrows and her skinning knife.

White Feather's task was the most difficult, for only she could recognize Red Fox, and she would have to be near to the camp to be certain. Proven warrior that she was, she silently parted the darkness, blending into the long shadows that moved with the moonlight and night breeze. She dropped to the ground, flattening herself below the bunch grass, and slithering close to the thick cottonwood grove. Her buckskin made no noise as she slipped over a downed branch and behind the twisted barkless cottonwood snag that stood like a black skeleton with leafless branches clawing at the night sky.

Joseph found the smooth sandstone promontory as Raven had directed and started to step up, but looked below to see the approaching figure of a warrior, working his way up the sliding sand and gravel to make it to the top. When he stood erect, he was startled by the appearance of Joseph, standing before him totally naked and growling, showing only his white teeth. Quills-in-Nose was frozen with fear, tried to step back away from this shadowy phantom, but found himself impaled on a lance. With eyes wide and mouth gasping for air, the warrior that had bragged he never knew fear, flapped his arms as if trying to take flight and fell to his knees. His head dropped to the shaft of the lance held by Joseph, watching as blood mixed with his drool coursed down his torso and pooled black against the sandstone.

HAD THEY WAITED ANY LONGER, everyone would be in their blankets, but women were still fussing with tireless children and left-over food was being packed away. White Feather scanned the village, moving only her eyes as she searched. No one looked familiar, some women had already slipped beneath their blankets. Suddenly, a man barked a question and Feather saw a tree-stump looking figure that she knew was Crazy Wolf, and he was speaking roughly to a young woman whose back was to Feather. He reached out and back-handed the girl, knocking her to her knees as she turned away. Feather immediately recognized Red Fox. Crazy Wolf started to kick at her, but she rolled away and jumped to her feet, answering Crazy Wolf with, "I will go, I will go," as she reached for a bladder bag used for water and she started for the river.

Red Fox staggered in the darkness, almost stepping on White Feather, but not seeing anything. She was focused on fetching the water and getting back before Crazy Wolf became even more angry and beat her or worse. White Feather crabbed back away from the tree, trying to reach Red Fox before she returned. Feather turned and crawled toward the girl, now bending at the water to fill the bladder. As Feather neared, she looked back at the camp, thought she was far enough away not to be seen and started to stand. Just then, Fox turned and saw the shadowy figure behind her and screamed. Feather quickly stepped to her, putting her had to her mouth and whispering, "Red Fox, I am White Feather!" But the alarm had been sounded, and twigs snapped and the pounding of running feet told of approaching Apache. Feather grabbed at Fox to pull her aside toward the alders, but Fox stumbled, and Feather had to drag her. Shielded by the darkness, the women dropped into the thick bushes and dared not even breathe.

Fox had dropped the bladder which was quickly found by the two women that came to see what she had screamed about. They looked at the water, turned around to search the bushes, but seeing nothing, they talked to one another, too softly to be understood by anyone nearby. But their motions toward the water showed they thought the girl had fallen in and maybe been swept away. One reached for the bladder, filled it, and the two walked back to the camp.

As soon as the two women were away from the water and approaching the camp, Feather and Fox started off toward the waiting Lizzie. When they approached, Lizzie stood and whispered to Red Fox, "I said we'd come!" The women hugged but were startled by a scream that came from the camp. Above them, standing on the crest of the shoulder of the mound, the figure of Joseph was standing before a small fire, waving a lance overhead and dancing with wild gyrations, accompanied by roars and screams imitating the black spirit of the Gans.

Feather looked at the Apache camp and saw women grabbing their children and retreating into the trees, trying to hide in the darkness away from this terrifying spectre. She saw that Crazy Wolf was not going to run away again, and heard him as he barked at Horse and motioned for him to follow. Feather watched Horse grab his lance and war shield, and run to catch up with the angered Crazy Wolf. She witnessed as a black arrow whispered past Wolf, making him jump aside and look behind as the arrow pierced the bull hide shield of Horse. Both men stopped and stared at the dropped shield and the black arrow protruding from a shield that could not be penetrated by any typical arrow of the Apache or any other tribe they knew.

Horse turned to flee and was stopped by the painted face of Raven, standing with upraised tomahawk as he screamed his war cry. Horse lifted his arm in defense, but the tomahawk never fell. Instead a long-bladed knife parted his ribs and twisted in his insides as Raven let his war cry pierce the blackness. Horse was a big man. He grasped the wrist of Raven, trying to extricate the blade as he snarled at his enemy. He planted his feet wide, and tried to slap away the arm of Raven, only to feel the blade twist again for vital organs. The broad chest of the man heaved, and he opened wide his mouth as if wanting to bite off Raven's head. But no sound came, and blood coursed from the corners of his lips. His hand that tried to remove Raven's, slipped on the blood from his chest. Raven felt the blow of the backhand against his chest, surprised at the strength of this dead man still standing. Raven brought the tomahawk in a sweeping arch down against the knee of the big man, causing him to cave to the side, and finally drop to the ground, to fall to his face in death.

Crazy Wolf saw the big man grappling with Raven and believed no one could best his friend, so he turned to again assault the mound and find out if this was a real Gans or someone else. He had just cleared the bit of timber, taken a few strides, and was stopped when a black arrow buried itself in the path before him. He stopped and spun around, looking for the one that sent the arrow at him and saw a white man slowly walking to him as he spoke in low tones, but loud enough for him to hear.

Tatum had been told by White Feather that Crazy Wolf did not understand white man talk, but that he did know some Comanche. So, Tatum spoke to him, snarling out the words in the Comanche he had learned from White Feather during his first visit to their village. He started, "You are Crazy Wolf. You dare to come to my village and take my women. Now I will have to kill you!"

Tatum saw Wolf grin and snatch his knife from his belt and drop into a fighter's crouch. Tatum reached behind his back and brought out the razor-sharp Bowie, spread his arms wide and began to move side to side, staring at the grinning Apache. Tatum had a quick thought, *I don't believe I'm doing this! What?!?* and Wolf lunged forward, extending his arm seeking out the belly of this white man.

Tatum sucked in his gut, stepped slightly aside, and brought the Bowie down on the arm of Crazy Wolf. Wolf jerked back and almost stumbled, caught himself and grabbed at his injured arm with the other hand, blood flowing over his fingers and he looked at the white man in surprise and anger. Dropping his free hand, he lowered his head and charged at this man that came with the Comanche, he swiped at Tatum's stomach, split the buckskin tunic and brought blood.

Tatum staggered backward, slipped on a stone, flailed out his arms to catch his balance, but his legs flew out from under him. The moon, waxing toward full, lifted its sleepy head above the bank of clouds just at Crazy Wolf threw himself at the downed white man, the light glinting off his blade. The break of light helped Tate time his move and lifted his legs just as the solid stump of a man left the ground. Tate's legs absorbed the impact and lifted the Apache over his head, crashing into a cholla. The Apache screamed and rolled away from the grasping tentacles of the cactus, thrashing and slashing to escape. His body was covered with the prickly barbs but he ignored the pain and spun to attack. Tate arched his back and jumped to his feet, spinning around just in time to catch the arms of Wolf. The cactus barbs caused Tate to wince, but he kept his grip, knowing if he slacked, the Apache would try to bury the knife in his chest. The two struggled and pushed against each other, teeth bared and grunting, muscles bulging, as the bulkier and more experienced Wolf began to push back Tate. The white man's moccasins slid in the sand, but Tate refused to yield, and sucked air for another push-back. He gritted his teeth, clenched his jaw, let the air slowly escape from his chest as he gave his all and began to make the crazed Apache slip backwards.

Feeling his foothold give, Wolf sought better purchase but that slight hesitation was all Tate needed. The lean white man startled Wolf with a growl that ended in a scream as Tate feinted with his knife, causing Wolf to look, giving just enough advantage to Tate. He brought the knife hand in a backward arc that made Wolf think he had won, but Tate used the momentum to bring the long wide blade swooping past his thigh and up into the belly of the warrior, plunging it under his ribs and ripping his heart and into his lungs. The Apache lifted to his toes trying to escape but lost his breath, stared at the messenger of death, tried to spew the bloody slime from his mouth, but slumped on the knife in death.

Tate let the weight of his adversary carry him to the ground as he snatched his knife from the chest of Crazy Wolf. He thumped to the ground as air left his lungs and the body was unmoving. The moment of silence and stillness was shattered by the screams of a horde of women charging the two warriors now standing side by side. They stared at the shadowy forms of knife and lance wielding women crashing through the brush and undergrowth in their attack.

Suddenly, White Feather stepped before the men, raised her arms and shouted in the Apache language, "Stop! Stop!" The charging crowd hesitated as this woman that had been in their village, shouted at them in their language. She continued, "We do not want to hurt you! We only came to take back the woman captive you know as Red Fox. Your warriors have fought bravely, but you do not need to die. We will leave, and you can have your young men help you to your winter camp to join your people."

The women looked at White Feather, turned to one another and spoke among themselves. One of their leaders, Little Flower, wife of Crazy Wolf, said, "Leave us. Take Red Fox and go. We will tend to our dead. Leave!"

Feather turned to Raven and Tate, nodded and motioned in the direction of the waiting Lizzie and Red Fox, and the three walked away under the white light of the now risen moon. When they reached the horses, Joseph was waiting, and all agreed to travel as far as they could to return to their home. It would be a long night, but it would be good to get far away from the Apache lands.

CHAPTER THIRTY
RETURN

RAVEN TOOK THE LEAD AND HEADED OUT DUE EAST. THE LOW-LYING saddle between the big Flat Top mesa and the Pinyon hills would take them on a direct route to the Sangre de Cristo mountains and the winter camp of the WhahaToya band of the Yaparʉhka Comanche. They were greeted by wide bands of orange and red clouds that silhouetted the granite topped mountains as the rising sun pushed back the cloak of darkness. Raven had ridden well ahead of the others and now stood beside his horse at the edge of the trees along the banks of the Rio Grande. He waved them forward and stood with one hand resting on the withers of his paint stallion that shook his head and dug the dirt before him with one hoof, showing his impatience with his owner. The greenery, showing in the clearing behind Raven, was the reason for the annoyance of the horse that was anxious for good graze.

Raven had taken a young buck that had bedded down near the river and rose for his morning drink just as the hunter approached. Now the carcass lay waiting to be dressed out and made ready for the morning's meal. After the past several days of hard travel and fighting, the clearing was a welcome sight, and everyone was anxious for a relaxing and leisure time. They quickly stripped saddles and packs,hobbled the horses and mule, and began the work of making a comfortable camp. It went without saying they were going to spend at least a day, maybe more, just recuperating. The animals seemed to sense the relaxed mood of the group and after their obligatory roll in the dust, they drank deeply of the slow-moving water, and started their graze of the last of the season grass.

The women tended to the deer, sliced off several choice cuts of meat, and began readying the other foodstuffs. Joseph had gathered several armloads of firewood and Tate started the fire with his flint and steel. Raven stacked the packs and lay aside the bedrolls and joined Tate at the fireside. The men drug three logs near the fire for seating, Tate and Raven now sat across from one another, using the logs as backrests rather than seats. With feet to the fire and legs stretched before them, the two men silently reminisced the previous day's events as they stared glassy-eyed before the flames.

Joseph quietly sat on the remaining log and looked from one man to the other and said, "I sho' am praisin' de' Lawd for givin' me back muh sister, yessuh! An' I wanna be thankin' bof' of you's fo' all you done too! Now, I know de' Lawd was da' one whut made it possible, but you two's was used by Him to git it done, so, I be thankin' you." He let his gaze rest on the flames as they licked at the sizzling steaks and he licked his lips in anticipation.

Raven looked at Tate and asked, "What this mean, praisin' de Lawd?"

Tate looked at his friend and began, "Well, Raven, what he is saying in his own way is that he believes God worked things out for us. What you call the Great Spirit, and some call the One Above or Manitou or other names, we believe is God. When he says he praises the Lord, he is talking about our Savior and God." He looked to Raven for a response, but the expression on his face showed thoughtfulness, so Tate continued, "Our God is told about in our Bible, that's the book you've seen me reading, the one in my saddle bags. That book tells us that God loves each of us, whether Indian, white man," explained Tate as he pointed to Raven and himself and then to Joseph, "or black man.

God loves each of us and more than that, He wants each one to, as you would say, 'cross over' into Heaven when we die. But," and he spoke strongly to emphasize what he was about to say, "none of us deserve to 'cross over' to Heaven, because we have all failed Him. So, to make it possible He tells us in His book how to do that."

Raven had moved to sit on the log and leaned forward to ask, "How? How do we do that? Cross over to this Heaven, I mean." Red Fox had edged closer and White Feather listened as she worked. Tate saw their interest and continued.

"Well He made it easy for us by explaining a few things. The first thing we need to know is that all of us, you, me, Joseph, the women, all of us, have sinned, or done wrong. Then He tells us that because of that, what we deserve is to be kept out of Heaven, or according to His book, we deserve," and he paused, searching for the right way to explain, "to be punished forever, or as your people tell it, to wander in the darkness forever. That's the price for our wrongdoing." Tatum paused, picked up a stick and tossed it into the flames, "But, He also made a way to escape that. He sent His son to pay that price for us, you know, like when we fight a battle for others. See, Jesus, God's Son, fought His battle for us by dying on the cross."

Raven interrupted, "What do you mean?"

Tate thought about it, trying to help Raven understand, and said, "Well, I know that sometimes, when the Comanche take captives, they tie them up to the trees and torture them because they are enemies. That's what Jesus did for us."

"He was tied and beaten and died? How did that help?"

"Because after He died, He came back to life to show us He paid for our wrongs. Now, if that happened when your people beat someone to death and he came back, wouldn't you let him go?"

Raven looked at Tate, then to the flames and said in a low voice, "Yes, we would believe the Great Spirit had brought him back and we would let him go."

"Well, when Jesus did that, He came back to show us what we should do. He said He had a gift for us, but we had to believe and accept that gift, and if we did, then when we die, we will 'cross over' and live in Heaven forever."

Raven looked at Tatum, examining his expression and trying to see into his heart and know his truthfulness, and asked, "This gift, to be able to cross over and live in Heaven, how do we get this?"

Tatum noticed that Red Fox was now resting on her knees, sitting back on her feet, just behind the log with Raven and leaned slightly forward, waiting to hear the answer. White Feather had stopped her work and stood listening. Tatum said, "It is not much different than when you speak to your Creator or Great Spirit, it's what we call prayer. And God's word, the Bible tells us that 'Whosoever shall call upon the name of the Lord, shall be saved.' So, if you truly believe what I've just told you, and you want to receive His gift, then just take time to pray and say something like, 'I believe in what Jesus did when He died for me and I ask for the gift of eternal life.'" Tate looked at each one and added, "It's not the words you say but what you feel here," motioning to his heart.

Raven slowly nodded his head, looked at White Feather and Red Fox, then back at Tatum and said, "This is good, what you say. I will think on this."

Joseph had quietly listened and slowly nodded his head to Tate, looked at his sister with a broad grin, and back at Tate, still grinning. Lizzie had been helping White Feather and reached down for the coffee pot, grabbed the cups and started toward the men to pour each of them a cup of the steaming brew. When she got to Tate, she lifted her eyes to her friend and said, "My Pap woulda liked whatchu done said. You's a good man, Tate."

THE GREY LIGHT of early morning found the small group on the trail heading due east across the flatland south of the San Luis hills. It was desolate and dry country and every step of the horses kicked little clouds of powder fine dust to settle on the myriad of cactus that carpeted the prairie floor. As the sun sought to bake them with its blistering rays of early winter, they rode hunch-backed, occasionally swatting at pesky flies and gnats that sought their salty sweat. A cool breeze from the snow dusted mountains brought brief relief, and they lifted their heads.

The sun had made short work of its passage across the cloudless sky and now sat upon the distant mountains splashing the sky with brilliant shades of gold. The travelers neared the edge of the black timber that trimmed the skirts of the Sangre de Cristo mountains and followed a small stream into the pines and found a suitable clearing, carpeted with a thick layer of long needles from the towering ponderosa. Raven had said the journey over the mountain pass would take another day, maybe two, before they would reach the winter camp of the Comanche and his home. White Feather and Red Fox had shown their eagerness to be among their people and Tate thought wistfully of his own home, the cabin in the mountains far to the north. But he thought, *Soon, pretty soon, at least it'll be soon if ol' man winter holds off.*

CHAPTER THIRTY-ONE
MOUNTAINS

THE NOTCH OR SADDLE BETWEEN THE TWO SMALLER PEAKS ON THE tail-end of the Sangre de Cristo mountains was an easily negotiated pass in the summertime. But this was the early part of a promising winter and when the travelers broke from the trees clearing timberline, the snow was blinding white in an unbroken expanse that stretched from mountaintop to mountaintop. Raven was in the lead with his high stepping paint stallion, breaking a trail through the accumulated snow. Later in the winter, this would be unpassable, but the dry snow of a cold fall had been blown about by the high-altitude winds. The stallion stumbled, and Raven caught himself with a hand on the horse's withers, then pushed back his weight to aid his horse in regaining his footing. Within just a few steps, they were free of the drift and on frozen tundra. He reined up to wait for the others and as Tate neared, he said, "It will be like this," and motioned with a sweep of his arm, "on the other side, but soon we will be in the trees. Then we can stop, have some of your coffee."

Tate chuckled at Raven, knowing he had scorned coffee until the first cold morning. After that, he wanted coffee every time they stopped. He wondered how much more this man would have enjoyed the coffee if he hadn't run out of sugar. He nodded his head to Raven, pulled the hood of the capote up and turned to check on the others. Within moments, the group was together and looking at the frozen tundra and granite slide rock they would have to cross. Raven nudged the paint forward and the others strung out to follow.

Raven gave the horse his head and the nimble paint picked his footing carefully. The tundra had short-cropped vegetation, although covered by a thin coat of ice, that gave better footing for the wary animals. But the slide rock, icy and unstable, was the challenge. Raven slipped off his horse and signaled for the others to do likewise. He led the horse with a long loose lead rope, giving the animal room to choose his own footing, but even then, the often-teetering slide rock, caused the horse to stop and search Tatum led his sorrel as he picked his own footing, often stumbling and catching himself with his mittened hands or his knees. Tatum was leading the sure-footed mule too and had no concern for him, but he was a little fearful for the others.

Raven stopped at a small tundra covered hummock and watched the others pick their way as they followed. Joseph and Lizzie followed Tate as Red Fox rode close behind them. White Feather was bringing up the rear and seemed to be climbing the trail without difficulty. As Joseph and Lizzie stopped beside Raven, Tate said to him, "You go 'head on, I'll wait for the others, then I'll follow after."

Raven nodded and started toward the saddle crossing. They were about sixty yards from the crest, but it would not be easy. More drifts blocked the way, but Tate hoped there would be enough snow to cover the slide rock, it would have better footing than the icy rock. He watched as Raven approached the first drift, paused and stepped into the snow. The crusty top of the drift gave way and Raven sunk to knee depth, forced another step, broke the crust again, and continued breaking trail through. Tate tiptoed to see that one more drift stretched across the trail before they would reach the crest. He watched as Joseph, Lizzie and Red Fox struggled with every step, but kept moving as they tugged at their mount's leads. He turned to see White Feather drop to her knees beside him, breathing heavily as she looked above at the rest of the trail. The thin mountain air made everyone gasp for breath, and the extra exertion easily sapped the strength and stamina from the climbers. White Feather's shoulders lifted and fell as she sucked air, but she soon struggled to her feet, forced a smile at Tatum as she said, "Fire, coffee, trees . . . " as she pointed to the crest. He grinned at her and motioned for her to lead off.

The biting wind that whistled over the saddle at the crest gave impetus to each one as they reached the high point and eagerly started their descent. The wind seemed to channel itself up the wide draw searching for the crest to blow itself out. The back side of the saddle like crossing was different only by the shelter from the wind. Drifts, slide rock, and icy tundra seemed to work in concert to discourage the group. They were tired, winded and sore from falling to their hands and knees on the slide rock. Their arms had been repeatedly jerked by the lead ropes of their mounts.

Raven was nearing the timberline and stopped to look back at the others. Joseph had just cleared the slide rock when he heard a shout and looked back to his sister, who was on her knees, looking back at her struggling mount. The horse was trying to gain footing, but one leg dangled at an awkward angle, apparently broken when it stumbled on the rock. Lizzie fearfully looked at the horse, down the slope at her brother, and back at the still struggling horse. The animal had gained footing for his good leg and now stood trembling, wide eyed, staring at the girl at the end of the lead rope. Lizzie was crying and sobbing, but valiantly worked her way back to the pony to try to give it comfort and to keep it from moving.

When the commotion began, Tatum looked below and saw the Indian pony that had held Lizzie, and heard the sobbing of the girl and he spoke to Feather, "Wait up, hold onto my horse. I need to get to Lizzie." Feather reached out a hand to take the lead-rope and nodded her understanding as Tatum hurried to help. He stepped from rock to rock, pushed through the broken trail of the drift, and was soon at the side of Lizzie. He put a hand on the rump of the horse as he walked alongside. Seeing the dangling foreleg, he said to Lizzie, "Go on down with your brother. I'll take care of this." She looked wide-eyed at her friend, reading his expression and dropped her face in her hands and muttered, "I'm sorry, I'm sorry."

"Go on now," directed a somber Tatum.

He stepped to the side of the trembling mare, loosened the latigo and dropped the saddle to the ground. He moved to the front of the horse, holding the reins tight, and rubbed the forehead of the animal, speaking softly. He slipped the Paterson Colt from the holster, put the muzzle to the side of the horse's head and pulled the trigger. The sharp report of the pistol echoed across the valley, startling everyone and the animals as well. The pony dropped and lay still. Tatum looked up hill to Red Fox and White Feather, motioned for them to come down and started back up the steep slope to retrieve his mount and the pack mule.

Lizzie doubled up with Joseph and the group soon made the timber, found an acceptable clearing amidst the thick fir and spruce, and gathered together for a warm fire and hot coffee. This would be a short stop for the animals to get some rest, and settle the nerves of both them and riders. The rest of the way would be easy going compared to what they just covered.

The rest of the day saw the group following a game trail that shadowed the creek bottom in the cleft between the mountains. Raven knew they would not make the winter camp of the Comanche before dark and chose to make camp when they found a clearing where the ravine widened. Tucked away amidst a cluster of tall light barked spruce, a small grassy meadow bordered the creek that offered both graze and water. They made an early camp and looked forward to a good meal and a comfortable night's rest. Tomorrow they would be at the Comanche camp.

As the women prepared the meal, Tatum wandered into the black timber, enjoying the quiet and the beauty of the woods. A cluster of kinnikinnick stubbornly held to its red berries and a bunch of low growing plants held dark red raspberries. He gathered the raspberries, using the shirt-tail of his buckskin shirt to hold them all, and looked around for other bounty. A chokecherry bush beckoned, and he added a couple of hands full of the ripe tidbit to his pouch. He wandered back to camp in time to bestow his gathered gift on the women. It was an ample supply for everyone to have a sweet treat to top off the hot meal and give an added touch of comfort to their time together.

TATUM LAY, hands behind his head, watching the big moon climb the dark sky and thought about the times he spent with his father looking at the stars and naming the constellations. He picked out several familiar figures in the stars, named them to himself and sucked in a lung full of cold mountain air. He smiled to himself, said a short prayer of thanksgiving, and rolled over for a good night's sleep.

CHAPTER THIRTY-TWO
COMANCHERIA

THE INDIAN SUMMER SUN HUNG LAZILY AT ITS HIGHEST POINT, unhindered by any cloud. The clear blue sky arched over the mountain valley and gave a welcome to the weary travelers. Raven rode side-by-side with Red Fox, trailed by the others, as they entered the village. There was a stir of excitement as the villagers recognized Raven, but they pointed at the girl, questioning who was this visitor, obviously Comanche, that rode with him. Suddenly a woman, a touch of grey at her temples, clasped her hands to her mouth and stood staring. Recognition painted her face and she stepped forward, calling the name, "Red Fox! Red Fox! My child!" as the girl slipped from her mount and wrapped her mother in a tight embrace.

She looked back at Raven, who sat smiling astride his paint, and she said, "My heart is glad. I am with my mother!"

The rest of the village made the group welcomed as Buffalo Hump greeted his son and daughter and bid Tatum and his friends a cheerful greeting. welcome. He immediately called for a feast to be given for the return of his family and the village soon hummed with excitement. Raven directed Tatum to a tipi for him, Joseph and his sister to use as their own during their stay and after the horses and mule were turned out with the village herd, the three soon made the lodge comfortable with their bedrolls and gear.

A short time later, a scratching at the entry flap gained White Feather entry to the lodge of the trio. She grinned at her friends and asked Lizzie, "What do you think of my village?"

"I neva' thought it'd be so big. But your people are real friendly!" declared Lizzie, excitedly. She never dreamed she would be in an Indian village as anything but a captive like she experienced with the Apache, and the experience was exciting and puzzling at the same time.

White Feather asked, "Would you like me to show you the rest of the village?"

Lizzie looked at her brother, he nodded, and she turned back to White Feather, "I'd like that a lot. Could Joseph come too?"

"Yes, and you could come as well," she said to Tatum.

Lizzie walked beside White Feather and Joseph and Tatum followed behind. As they walked the perimeter of the village, many of the villagers stared and Lizzie began to show a bit of nervousness when she asked, "They lookin' at us kinda funny like. What they gonna do?"

White Feather chuckled and said, "Many of my people have never seen a person with dark skin like you and your brother. They do not know about you."

Joseph said, "They don't think like the Apache, do they. I mean, they don't think I be some kinda spirit or nothin'?"

White Feather looked at both her friends and said, "No, not as a spirit. But, you are different, and they wonder why. It will take time for them to understand, but no harm will come to you."

As they neared the end of their circuitous tour, a naked young boy came up to White Feather, pointed at Lizzie and asked, "Why is she dark?" The boy had spoken in Comanche and was not understood by Lizzie, but she guessed what was said and watched as Feather tried to explain. When Feather pointed at Lizzie, the girl stepped forward and held out her hand for the boy to see. He looked up at her, slowly raised his hand and touched hers, looked at his and touched her again. He lifted his eyes to hers, smiled, and ran away.

White Feather explained, "He just asked about your skin and when I told him it was no different than ours, he asked to touch you to be sure. You were kind to let him touch you."

Lizzie replied, "I could tell what he was thinkin' an' I'se glad to hep' him unnerstand. If everbody just tried to unnerstand we be no different, things'd be better ever'where."

White Feather hugged her friend and said, "I will come back to go with you to the feast."

THE CENTRAL COMPOUND was ringed with tipis, all with the entry facing the East and the first light of the day. Several cookfires had many women busy with the feast preparation with a wide variety of meats and gathered wild vegetables ranging from onions to potatoes and more. A large fire ring in the middle of the compound held a small fire, but stacks of wood nearby lay in anticipation of a large festive blaze for the celebration. Men had begun to gather in the compound and some had arranged their willow backrests in choice places with buffalo robes and other blankets nearby. Others would take their place after the chief chose his and would be arranged according to their position within the band. Near the chief would be his family and special guests, and then the sub-chiefs would take their places.

White Feather scratched at the entry flap and was quickly greeted by Lizzie as she stepped from the lodge. She was followed by Joseph and Tatum and the eager group walked quickly to the compound. Buffalo Hump had taken his place with Raven at his side with reserved places beside them. Tatum was pointed to the place near Raven. Joseph and Lizzie were given the place beside White Feather, who sat next to her father. These were places of honor for the guests of the chief because custom required the guests to be given the same honor and treatment given to the chief and his family.

They were no sooner seated when the women began to serve,

starting with the chief and then to the others. They were handed carved bark platters, well mounded with an assortment of meats and other foodstuffs. Their only utensils were their fingers, or if they preferred, the knife at their belt. Tate set the example Joseph and Lizzie followed as they dug into their meal. Conversation was minimal while they ate, but Lizzie repeatedly asked Feather about the different foods, receiving simple and sometimes curt answers. Finally, she asked, "Is it wrong for me to speak or ask y'all questions?"

Feather looked at her inquisitive friend and smiled, answering, "It is not wrong, for I know you want to learn. But most believe that when we eat, we should eat. And when we talk, we talk."

Lizzie returned the gaze of her friend, looked to her platter, and back to Feather, nodded her head and focused on her food. Joseph had been content to enjoy the meal, for he was never one to question food, as long as he had plenty l, he was content. As each one finished their meal, the platters were set aside to be gathered by the women in attendance, and conversation began. The tradition of the people was to use this time for the telling of stories, usually stories of recent feats or adventures. At the encouraging of his father, Buffalo Hump, Raven stood to tell the story of the rescue of Red Fox.

As Raven began his telling of their plan and the actions of the small group beginning with the role played by Joseph as the dreaded black Gans, he did so with considerable dramatization and elucidation, gaining the attention of all the listeners. Repeatedly, the crowd erupted in laughter as Raven pretended to be Joseph in his gesticulations and dancing. During the entire tale, White Feather quietly translated for Joseph and Lizzie, much to the delight of both. After he finished with the details of the fight between him and Horse, and the fight of Tate and Crazy Wolf, the crowd had grown quiet and somewhat mesmerized at the bravery shown by all the visitors, that they had done this to rescue one of their own.

When Raven finished with his storytelling, many of the people made their way around the circle to speak to each of the group. Sometimes they were given nothing more than a nod and a pat on the back, other times they were greeted with considerable expressions of respect and appreciation. This was great honor given from the people to these that were not of the Comanche, and Tate, Joseph and Lizzie were pleased and somewhat surprised.

There were other stories told of the recent battle and the individual honors earned by the many warriors that were there, but the storytelling time soon waned. Some of the women began building up the central fire in preparation of the coming dance. A large bull-hide drum was brought out and several men gathered around and began beating out a rhythm and chanting. Suddenly, a lone figure jumped into the firelight, startling many as he began shouting and chanting. He was garbed in a breechcloth, bone and beaded breastplate, a cape of buffalo hide, and a head dress of feathers and tufts of various colors. His face was painted, and he began to dance in a crouch, lifting high his legs and feet that were adorned with high-topped beaded and fringed moccasins and small bells. He brandished a ceremonial lance with feathers, scalps and strips of leather braided and hanging in long fringe. Every move was exaggerated and he double-stepped, forward and backward, side to side, always moving, always chanting. Everyone watched as he moved around the central fire, the flames casting shadows sometimes reaching higher than the nearby lodges, magnifying the mesmerizing movements of the dancer. Soon many others joined the dance and pantomimed their part in the recent battle with moves of stealth and attack.

As the first dancer came near the group of guests, he would face each one, still dancing and chanting, waving his lance, seeming to taunt the visitors. When he neared Tatum, he focused on him, emphasizing his movements and threatening taunts, screaming louder as he chanted. It was then that Tatum recognized the archenemy from his past, Spirit Talker, the shaman of this band of Comanche. He watched the taunts and threats of the shaman, never moving nor changing his expression to show anything but mild interest.

The Comanche believe the spirits of the dead did not leave, but were still with them, moving about their camp and lodges, often intervening in their lives. This belief gave them room to blame the spirits for accidents or illness and to determine their choices in life. But the appearance of a spirit from the past is never considered, believing the spirits intentionally remain invisible so they can do their work. But the thought of the spirits of the departed was not in Tatum's mind as he watched this man that openly threatened him during his dance.

As the dancer continued his circuit of the fire, he disappeared from the view of Tatum and the others. When he suddenly reappeared, his feather headdress had been replaced with what had been the top skull and cape of a bull buffalo, black horns protruding threateningly from the sides. The thick brown fur on top of the skull cap and cascading down the back of his neck to his shoulders and below, bounced with the movements of his dance. When the people of the village saw this figure, they thought they were seeing the spirit of Black Buffalo, the man who was the shaman before Spirit Talker and had died during the smallpox epidemic. Black Buffalo, the shaman at the time, had been a friend and helper with Tatum during the epidemic. But Spirit Talker, Black Buffalo's successor, blamed Tatum for the death of his mentor. If was because of the threats of Spirit Talker that Tatum left the village before and now the man was again threatening the white man he hated.

When Spirit Talker continued his menacing dance, mimicking a warrior attacking an enemy, he approached the group seated with Buffalo Hump. His hatred and venom fired his zeal and he forgot the custom of his people to treat the guests of the chief with honor, and started toward Tatum, with the lust of vengeance burning in his eyes. His charge brought Buffalo Hump, Raven and Tatum to their feet. Before he could reach Tatum, Raven slapped the lance aside, tripped the shaman, causing him to fall on his face at the feet of his enemy.

He scrambled to his feet, snarled at Raven, threatening him, "You dare to strike your shaman?! You will be cursed by the spirits!!" he screamed.

Buffalo Hump stepped before him and in a strong but even voice he intimidated the out-of-control shaman into submission as he said,

"You have brought shame to this village! This man is my guest and you dare to threaten him?" The chief stretched out his arm and pointed to the lodge of the shaman and ordered, "Go and examine your own heart. You will not bring the spirits to bear on my son or my guest! You will stay in your lodge, or you will be banished from this village forever!"

Spirit Talker jerked the buffalo headdress from his head, snarled toward Tatum, and stomped away. Buffalo Hump turned to Tatum and said, "This man has shamed me and my village. You are our guest and our custom demands you be treated with respect and honor. You have helped my people, fought beside us against our enemy, and been a friend."

Tatum reached out his arm, clasped forearms with the chief and said, "You and your people will always be my friends. You have honored me and my friends," nodding toward Joseph and Lizzie, "with this feast and your friendship. The man who was shaman during my first visit, was also my friend and spoke with some concern about Spirit Talker. He did not believe this man would be a good shaman, and he hoped to choose another, but he was taken too soon. We will leave with the first light of tomorrow, until then my friend, we will go to our lodge."

Tatum motioned for Joseph and Lizzie to join him and the three returned to the lodge. Before they settled in, a scratch at the entry and the voice of White Feather told of her presence. Lizzie called for her to come in and the four were soon seated before the hearth in the center of the tipi.

"You said you were leaving tomorrow?" asked Feather.

"Yeah, as you know, we've got lots to do before ol' man winter sets in," explained Tatum.

Lizzie looked to her friend and said, "I wish you was comin' wid' us, Feather. There's a lot more for me to learn from you!"

"I would love to teach you everything I know, my friend. But I must stay with my people. I am needed here." She looked at Lizzie and casually glanced up at Tatum. He dropped his eyes to the fire, thinking.

Joseph said, "It won't be the same wid'outchu, White Feather. You been dere longer'n we have. 'Sides, we fixed up the wickiup fer me'n Tate, an' you'n Lizzie's to use da' cabin. If'n you don't come, she gonna be all 'lone."

Feather looked at the others around the fire and let her gaze linger on Tatum, who sat silently with eyes on the flames. She started to rise, and Tatum said, "You are my best friend. You have helped us all and we would like to have you with us, if you will."

Now standing, she looked at her friend and replied, "If I am not here when you leave tomorrow, go in peace." She smiled at each one and slipped out of the lodge.

CHAPTER THIRTY-THREE
SHAMAN

Tatum's own call to freedom brought images of his cabin in the Sangre and stirred him to wakefulness before first light. He lay still under the heavy buffalo robe, searching the darkness to get his senses about him. He slowly slipped from under the cover. He moved silently to the entry, pushed the flap aside and stood before the tipi. He stretched his stiff muscles as he lifted his eyes to the starlight looking at the moon slowly dropping its distorted shape to the Western horizon. A tinge of color showed to the east, but Tatum knew it would be a while before the sky would begin to grey. He walked to the edge of the village to tend to his morning constitutional, moving quietly on the pine needle carpet.

When he returned, he stopped at the edge of the trees, looked at the conical shadows of the village, and thought about White Feather. *I wonder if she'll come with us, she's good company, and right nice to look at too.* He shook his head at his wandering thoughts, dropping his eyes to the ground.

A whisper of movement caught his attention and he looked up just in time to see the glint of the starlight on the blade of an upraised knife. He jerked back into the trees, stumbling as he moved, kicking out at his attacker. His foot caught the would-be assailant at the side of the knee and caused him to stagger into the low branch of the ponderosa. Tatum scrambled to his feet, grabbing at the knife in the scabbard at his back. He dropped into a crouch as the shadowy figure began to step toward him. With the dim light of pre-dawn at his back, he appeared only as a black shadow and Tatum could not identify him. For a guest of the chief to be attacked in the village was totally against the custom of the people and Tatum could only think of one man that would dare to go against the will of his chief, Spirit Talker!

The shaman emitted a growl from deep in his chest"You will die! It is the will of the spirits!" He lunged forward only to have Tatum step quickly aside and bringing his knife in a slapping move against the face of his attacker. Tatum did not want to kill this man, he was important among the Comanche and Tatum held no animosity against him, but he had to defend himself. Now the positions were reversed, Tatum's back was to the dim light that now showed on the eastern skyline, and what light pierced the trees showed the still-painted face of the angry shaman. Instead of attacking, Tatum began to back-step away from the trees, giving more light and more room for the fracas. He moved slowly, carefully, remembering the last time he backed up in a fight and slipped on a rolled rock that almost cost him his life.

The shaman, now in a crouch and swinging his knife side to side, snarled at the hated man, "You have shamed me, for this you must die!"

"You shamed yourself, Spirit Talker, you shoulda left well enough alone," answered Tatum as he started to move in a circular pattern, always to the right of his attacker. If he could catch him off balance, weight on the near foot, maybe he could get his knife hand and disarm him. The two moved as two mountain lions facing each other, carefully picking each step, never taking their eyes off the other. Spirit Talker feinted, backed off and took another step, warily watching for a chance to strike. Tatum kept his distance, never dropping the tip of the big Bowie, moving it slightly to keep Talker's attention. Tatum feinted, making the shaman shift his weight away and Tatum connected with his balled fist against the shaman's ear. Talker was slightly stunned, but kept his feet, even lunging forward with his knife. Tatum sucked his gut in, stretched on his toes, and barely escaped the blade, but on the back swing his tunic was sliced open and he felt the burn of a cut on his side.

The fight caught the attention of a warrior coming back from the woods and the alarm went through the camp. People began to come near to see what the commotion was all about. All were surprised to see their shaman, a man whose position kept him from battle, in a fight with the white man. But after the display of the previous night, they understood what was happening.

The fight continued with one swiping attack after another, neither gaining the advantage. Tatum's side was bleeding, but not badly and the shaman showed no blood. Again, the shaman feinted, but Tatum didn't move away, surprising the attacker. Each time before, when the shaman feinted, Tatum would move to the side, leaving himself open for another lunging attack. But Tatum had watched for a pattern to his moves, knowing the shaman would try to bring his knife forward as Tatum stepped aside, but this time Tatum did not move. As the shaman stepped forward for his attack, Tatum caught at the man's wrist with his free hand, moving the blade away, and brought the blade of the Bowie under the man's arm, and slicing the muscle at his side. He could have as easily driven the blade between his ribs, but he didn't want to kill this leader of the comanche.

The shaman screamed at the wound, grabbing at it with his free hand that came back bloody, angering the attacker more. Now driven by his lust for blood, he raised the knife high and charged at Tatum as he screamed. But the whisper of an arrow that flew past Tatum and buried itself in the chest of the shaman stopped the man as if he hit a wall. The shaman lifted to his toes, grabbed at the arrow as he looked at the fletching of the shaft, then lifted his eyes to see the face of the man holding the bow, Buffalo Hump, his chief. The shock registered in his eyes and the light of life left them. He tottered a step and fell forward, the impact driving the arrow through his chest to protrude from his bloody back as a marker of failed vengeance.

The gathered crowd stood spellbound and silent, looking at their chief. They knew their leader had only done what honor demanded and they did not fault him. That was what was expected, even demanded of a leader.

Buffalo Hump walked slowly to the side of his friend, Longbow, placed his hand on his shoulder and said, "He had shamed us, you are our friend." With head bowed, he walked away, not looking back. Tatum stood tall, sucking air from his exertion and relief, and turned to the lodge of his friends.

As he stepped into the tipi, Joseph and Lizzie had just crawled from their bedrolls and looked up at the haggard Tatum. Joseph asked, "What happened? You look terrible!"

He stood with the knife still clutched at his side and showing blood, he lifted it, wiped the blade on the corner of a blanket and slipped the Bowie back in its sheath at his back. He dropped to his knees on the buffalo robe and sat back on his heels and shared the story of the fight and death of the shaman. Lizzie grew wide-eyed at the telling and Joseph asked, "So, we still leavin'?" Tatum looked up at his friend, nodded his head, and reached to roll the robes for traveling.

They had gathered their gear and stacked most of it outside and were finishing up with the rest of their packing when a familiar scratching at the entry admitted White Feather. Lizzie looked up and smiled as she said, "Are you comin' wid' us?"

White Feather stood quietly, looking from one to the other and said, "I was going to come, I had decided to spend the winter with my friends. But now I cannot."

"But why? Why can'tchu come? We want you to come," pleaded Lizzie. Joseph and Tatum looked at one another and both turned to White Feather.

She dropped her head and began to explain, "Spirit Talker was our shaman. Both Spirit and I studied with Black Buffalo and he was chosen to become the shaman when Black Buffalo was gone. But now,

Spirit Talker has crossed over and our people need a new shaman. My father, Buffalo Hump, has said that there is no one else. It is a great honor that I have been chosen for and I cannot leave my people."

Tatum dropped his head and spoke softly, "So, it's my fault that you can't come with us. If I hadn't fought with the man, you would be." He shuffled his feet, frustrated with himself, and added, "I tried not to kill him, but he kept coming. When the chief shot that arrow, I was relieved that I didn't have to kill him, but now . . . "

"It is no fault of yours. Spirit Talker was blinded by his jealousy of what you did for our people, and he was threatened by you. You have done no wrong, my friend." She looked at Tatum and added, "My heart is heavy for you, but this must be as I have said. You will always be my friend and a friend of our people." She dropped her head, turned away and stepped from the lodge.

The three friends stood silently as they thought about what was to be, Tatum broke the silence as he said, "Well, we need to be movin', got a long ways ta' go."

CHAPTER THIRTY-FOUR
RIDE

THE TRIO TRAVELED IN SILENCE, THEIR MINDS AND HEARTS A JUMBLE AS they thought of those that had become such good friends. The past several days had some of the most challenging for everyone, and the events of the past year had been far beyond the expectations of the young people. But now they were relieved to be headed to what had become their home, the simple cabin in the mountains. Just the thought of the safety and warm cabin brought comfort to them all. Tatum, now in the lead of the small caravan, stood in his stirrups and turned back, speaking loud enough for both Lizzie, directly behind him, and Joseph, off to the side, to hear as he said, "It's sure gonna be good to get home! I'm hopin' we got 'nuff time 'fore the heavy snows come to get ever'thin' done. How 'boutchu?"

Joseph grinned as he said, "Yassuh! I'se lookin' to sit by the fire and reeelax! No more dancin' on the mountain and chasin' after Injuns!"

Lizzie laughed at the two men and said, "Well, leastways you two didn't hafta be no captive o'them injuns! I had 'nuff o' bein' a slave 'fo' we came outchere, dint' want no mo' of it. We s'pose to be free!"

Tatum, again turned around in his seat to look back at his friends, said, "It's what they call frontier freedom Lizzie. Sumpin' ya' gotta fight for ever' day. If'n the Indians don't take it from you, the critters or the mountains will. Freedom ain't easy, ain't never easy."

The trail paralleled the Cucharas River through the valley East of the Sangre de Cristo range. This was familiar country for Tatum, the same country he first explored when he came to the mountains and spent time with the Comanche. He thought of the folks from the wagon train and the epidemic of smallpox, a time he didn't like to remember. He stood in his stirrups to survey the valley beyond, it opened a little wider and a bit of meadow stretched away from the river toward the forest of pine and spruce. A small herd of elk was grazing, unconcerned about any danger as they basked in the warm sunlight and deep grass. Tatum held up his hand to stop those behind, turned in his seat and spoke softly, motioning with a nod of his head, "There's some elk yonder, I think I'll try for one with my bow. Joseph, you come back me up with the Hawken and Lizzie, you take care of the animals." He slipped from his saddle, Joseph following, and they moved to the edge of the trees to start their stalk. Lizzie took the leads of the horses and mule, moved nearer the river and a wide patch of grass before finding a seat in the shade to wait.

"I'm gonna try for that spike bull there, behind the big one," whispered Tate, pointing out the intended target. Joseph nodded his head and stepped near the tall spruce to use as a rest, and motioned to Tate that he was ready. Tatum stepped into his bow, bringing the weapon to full draw, sighted along the shaft and let the arrow fly. It whispered on its way, singing through the air and found its mark before the animals had a chance to react. The young bull jerked away from the impact just behind his front leg and low in his chest. He tried to jump but only managed a couple of steps, staggered to his knees and fell to the side, unmoving. The rest of the herd sprang like they were connected by an invisible wire and vaulted away with the massive bull leading to the black timber.

. . .

LIZZIE HAD JUST SETTLED down to her comfortable seat, expecting a few moments of quiet solitude, when she heard the call of Joseph, summoning her to bring the animals to the site of the kill. When she arrived, the men had the butchering well under way with a gut-pile pulled to the side and the animal spread-legged with its entire carcass split from tail to tongue.

"We'll take the back-straps and the four quarters, leave the rest. The mule can only pack so much, so we'll need to split up some of the packs among the rest of us. But this elk'll make good eatin' tonight when we camp!" declared Tatum, standing with bloody hands and grinning. Joseph set-to and transferred some of the packs to the other horses, making room for the fresh meat of the elk. Within just a short while, the trio was back on the trail, enjoying the scenery of the wilderness valley and the mountains rising on both sides. It was beautiful country, but as Tatum already knew, it could be deadly country and he was anxious to get home. But it would take the rest of this day and all the next before they would reach their longed-for destination.

As the day wore on, Tatum noticed a slight drop in the temperature and began watching the sky. Clouds were piling up above the mountains to the far north and west, with shades of grey in the midst, Tatum began thinking they might be carrying snow. The farther they traveled, the darker the clouds that moved and danced as they seemed to walk across the mountains. A cold breeze licked at his face and he began to search for a camp for the night. He wanted to be in the trees for more protection from the wind, but not so deep as to be trapped by the deeper snow. With this wind, the flats would catch the snow, but it would be blown aside to be trapped by the ravines, gullies, and thick timber. If they were to travel, they had to stay in the open. But for now, they needed a wind-protected camp. He spotted what looked like an opening to a clearing and reined his horse toward the trees. He nodded to himself as he surveyed, noting the thick stand of spruce and aspen would be a good wind break. He motioned to the others to make camp.

Tatum began cutting saplings to form a lean-to shelter while

Joseph and Lizzie tended to the other camp chores. When Tatum pointed to the darkening clouds and told of his concern about a coming snow, they quickly set-to and within a short while all were enjoying fresh elk steaks and cornmeal biscuits. They picketed the horses along the side of the clearing with the thicker tree cover. The lean-to was nearby and the packs and gear were covered. They had close quarters in the lean-to, but no one complained, but each was hoping the storm would quickly pass and the next day's travel would be unhindered. As they stretched out in their bedrolls, Tatum asked, "So, Joseph, what are the two of you thinkin' come spring? You gonna hang around these mountains or you thinkin' of travelin'?"

"Don't rightly know, muh friend. I like dese mountains, but dey sure is a lotta Injuns," he declared.

Lizzie chimed in and said, "If dey was all like White Feather it'd be O.K., but they ain't."

Tate chuckled and said, "Well, you're right about that. But wherever you go, folks'll be the same, no matter what color they are, red, white, or black. There's always gonna be some that wanna take advantage of others. That happened to me back in Missouri, when my Pa was killed. Those folks that had been friends before, well, they wanted me gone in a hurry." He paused as he remembered the treatment he received after his father's death. What had been the home provided for the schoolmaster and his son, was taken away They said they needed it for the next schoolmaster even though they had done nothing to get one yet. But he was also thankful that gave him the excuse to head west to fulfill the dreams he and his pa shared. Now he was sleeping under the stars in the mountains.

"Well, you two will always have a home where we are now. Even if I decide to go explore some more of the mountains, it'll still be just as much your home as mine."

"You thinkin' 'bout leavin'?" asked Joseph, propping himself up on his elbows to look at Tatum.

"Well, not now! Not until at least next spring, maybe not then. But someday I want to see *all* the Rocky Mountains!"

"That's a lotta lookin'," said Lizzie as she turned to look at her friend. Darkness was settling into the trees and the wind whistled through the pines whipping the branches and moving the snags to creak and snap like demons in the darkness. The horses, growing a little nervous, stomped their feet and mumbled their concerns through their noses. The sounds of the night made the trio restless and little sleep was to be had until well after midnight when the wind settled down and the forest grew still. And the snow began.

CHAPTER THIRTY-FIVE
BLIZZARD

THE SNOW DRIFTED OVER THE BIG BUFFALO ROBE THAT COVERED THEIR feet, the wind had sculpted the drift around the front of the lean-to and left a sharp edge on the overhead edge of the lean-to with a slight overhang that taunted the sleepers as they stirred with the morning quiet. The wind had let up in the night, but the snow continued to fall, and the light breeze did the work of building the drifts. Now as the white sparkled in the fading moonlight and the dark gave way to the coming dawn, the wind began again. Tatum threw back his covers,and grabbed the Hawken that lay under the saddle he used for a pillow. He knelt on the buffalo robe, peering out into the white wilderness that sparkled with the new fallen snow. He looked to the horses and saw they had stomped the snow around them as they huddled together as best they could on the picket line. He stretched to look out from under the lean-to and scan the sky, seeing a low-hanging cloud cover that threatened more snow as a few flakes fell from the surrounding trees.

"We got a little break in the storm, we best be getting' on, 'fore it picks up again. Don't wanna get caught in the deep snow in these hyar trees. They tell me it can get deeper'n a fella's armpits and stay that way till spring. If it's all the same to you, I'd just as soon spend the winter in a nice warm cabin."

Joseph and Lizzie had been awakened by the first movements of Tatum and now listened as he railed against the weather, but when he spoke about a nice warm cabin, they both were motivated to get a move on. Joseph agreed, "Yassuh, a nice warm cabin do sound invitin', it do."

"We gots some biscuits and meat left from las' night. I'll round 'em up whiles ya'all get the horses ready. We can do wid'out coffee this one time. But I'll be sure'n make it easy to get to when we takes a break," answered Lizzie.

Without answering, Tatum stretched from the lean-to and started for the horses. The packs had been stacked and covered nearby so he started brushing the snow free as he reached for the gear. Joseph quickly joined him, dragging a couple of saddles from the lean-to and began saddling the horses. Tatum frigged his horse, slipped the Hawken in the scabbard, secured his bow to the pack, tied his bedroll behind his saddle and looked to the others. He suggested, "We prob'ly oughta have the robes or blankets handy, in case the storm worsens. Might need 'em to keep warm."

They traveled near the tree line with Tatum in the lead and his long-legged sorrel breaking trail. It was fairly easy going, the snow was light and a little less than a foot deep. The few drifts were small but by staying near the tree line, there were few to bust. About mid-morning they came to the confluence of the Cucharas River, Middle Creek and Abeyta Creek. This was where the wagon road nestled in the shadow of the big white ridge and led up and over the pass that would take them into the San Luis valley. It also brought memories flooding back of the wagon train with the Italian immigrants with smallpox.

Tatum had been watching the clouds as they continued to drop and turn dark, the lightly falling snow began to show bigger flakes and the wind began to pick up even more. As they took to the wagon road, the wind whistled down the valley that held the road that paralleled the creek in the bottom. They had traveled less than a mile on the road when the storm became horizontal. The wind blew the snow directly into the faces of the travelers as they hunched their shoulders into their coats, pulled their hats and hoods down over their foreheads and tugged scarves up over their faces. Tatum suddenly stopped and dropped from his saddle. He walked back to Lizzie's horse, pulled the lead rope from over the neck of the horse and tied it to the tail of the mule. He walked to Joseph's horse and did the same, tying the lead to the tail of Lizzie's horse. He leaned into the wind, keeping a hand on the horses as he forced his way back to his, brushed the snow from the saddle and stepped aboard. He nudged his horse forward and the sorrel complied, head hanging low as he plowed through the snow. Blankets were wrapped tight around the riders' shoulders, and they trusted the horses to keep to the roadway.

Within a short distance, the roadway did a switchback to climb the mountain to their left. With thicker timber and the wind at their backs, there was relief for rider and mount alike. The wind had blown the roadway clear and the going was easy until they neared the crest. As the road rounded the knob of the hill, the blowing snow released its full wrathThe wind pelted their faces with thick snowflakes that felt more like ice crystals. The horses struggled forward with the only advantage being the clear roadway. For the next two miles, the timber and wind worked in concert to keep the road clear and the travel a little easier, but soon they broke into the face of the storm.

It was difficult to even see the roadway, with snow and ice clinging to eyebrows and eyelashes, and the cold wind bringing water to their eyes. Ss they blinked it away, it turned to ice on their cheeks. Lizzie and Joseph squeezed their eyes shut, covered their faces with the edge of their blankets, and trusted the horses, now tethered together, to get them through the storm.

With brief glimpses of the roadway between the gusts of wind, Tatum managed to keep them on course. After cresting the pass, the road began its descent into the valley, but the cut between the mountains acted like a funnel for the blowing snow and the fury of the storm increased. When his sorrel stumbled the second time, and Tatum almost went over his head, the man stepped down and began to lead the group, breaking trail as he went. The wind blew the snow, but without any nearby trees, it began to accumulate in great swoops across the road way. Time and again, Tatum had to plow through by kicking at the snow, lifting his feet high and stomping the drifts, and sometimes they were so deep, he had to use his mittened hands to push his way through. His horse would make it with leaps and bounds, humping his back, lifting his forefeet and leaping forward after Tatum. It was the bond between horse and rider that made the animal trust this man that was leading him into the face of this icy blizzard.

A brief lull in the storm gave Tatum a quick glimpse of the mountains of the Sangres and the towering snow-capped peak of Mount Blanca showed itself against a patch of distant blue sky. Tatum turned toward the mountain, leaving the roadway and trusting his gut to keep him on course when the wind brought another icy blast at his face. He ducked his head and pushed on, picturing the black timber skirt of Mount Blanca and the shelter that timber would afford. He followed the slope of the hillside, knowing this would be hard going with the many ravines that cut their way from the peak to the valley beyond, but this was their best hope.

It was late afternoon when the storm seemed to have blown itself out of the valley, and continued its southward trek toward the lower hills of New Mexico territory. They had taken shelter in a deep ravine that gave respite from the wind and blowing snow, and now Tatum stood, looking Heavenward and saw the clouds breaking and a bit of blue trying to force its way through. He climbed the bank of the ravine, and looked around. The entire mountain held a blanket of white that began to sparkle as a few shafts of sunlight found their way through the clouds. He stretched as he looked around and then hollered to the two below, "Hey, let's get a move on, we can make the trees and some shelter 'fore dark! We can even have a fire!"

He slid down the embankment, tightened the cinch on his saddle, checked the rig on the mule and waited while Lizzie and Joseph checked their gear as well. Within moments, the trio was once again on the trail towards home. Tatum looked around, getting his bearings and thought, *If we just stop for some eatin' and a bit of rest. Keep goin' by the moonlight, we could make it 'fore mornin'! But maybe it'd be best to get some rest and do it tomorrow. The horses are purty tired, and I am too. Hummm, we'll see 'bout that when we stop.*

CHAPTER THIRTY-SIX
HOME

TATUM THOUGHT HOT COFFEE NEVER TASTED SO GOOD AS HE HELD THE hot cup wrapped in his hands and felt the steam rise against his face. He savored the aroma and sipped again at the brew, feeling it course its way down his throat, warming him as it traveled. They sat around the fire, soaking up every bit of heat they could as they stared at the flames, remembering how cold they were just a short while before. Tatum looked at the horses, now standing three-legged, eyes closed. They had struggled valiantly through the storm and deserved a good long rest, convincing Tatum to stay the night in this cozy camp in the thick spruce. The grassy clearing was almost clear of snow and the horses had rolled in the grass once they were free of the entanglement of the gear. They cropped the brown grass, savoring the food and now rested. Tatum looked from Joseph to Lizzie and asked, "You ever been in a storm like that'n'?"

"Wal, we had snow storms afore, but we didn't do no ridin' in 'em. We had 'nuff sense to come in outta da' storm!" declared Joseph, grinning.

"We're outta da' storm, ain't we?" asked Tatum of his friend, also grinning.

"Neither one's you'ns got 'nuff sense to come in outta no storm!"

declared Lizzie. "If'n it'd been up ta' me, we'd still be back in that nice warm tipi wid' White Feather, but no, you'ns wanted to git back to that rickety cabin." She grinned at the men, shaking her head.

"Well, if we don't have another blizzard like the one today, we should be home before dark tomorrow. I'm anxious to finish up with things, 'fore the winter really sets in," surmised Tatum.

"So, what all we gots to be doin'?" asked Joseph.

"Well, we might need to get more meat, but the main thing is to check out the roof, make sure we don't have any leaks. Also, the chinking with the moss and mud 'tween the logs and sealin' up 'round the windows. You know, little things like that. I'm sure we'll find other things to do as well."

"Now that White Feather ain't gonna be here, we still gonna use the wickiup?" asked Lizzie.

"Well, mebbe we can make do with just the cabin. We'll see," said Tatum, letting his thoughts drift to the cabin and the absence of White Feather. She would be missed, she had been a part of every-thing about the cabin and the life he was making in the wilderness. He heaved a heavy sigh, tossed a stick into the fire and said, "Maybe we better turn in, get some rest 'fore the last part of this trip."

IT WAS early afternoon when the mountainside just north of the Sand Dunes showed the familiarity of home. The day's travel had not been without challenges, snowdrifts and trail breaking, but with a blue sky and clear day, it had been a pleasant overall. Now as they approached the trail that would lead to the cabin, excitement rose in their chests and Tatum nudged the sorrel into the trees to find the trail. They quickly ascended to the clearing and the cabin and Tatum was ready to shout for joy when they broke from the trees. But the sight that greeted him brought him to a sudden halt and took his breath from him.

When they left, they had made a barrier of brush, rope, and lodge-poles that circled the clearing, providing ample grass and water from the small stream that came from the cavern for the two mules left behind. At one end of the clearing, the barrier had been torn down, and lying in the middle of the clearing was the remains of the carcass of one of the mules. The wickiup had been torn apart and had nothing more than a skeleton of bent ridge poles standing. Claw marks marred the logs by the doorway and the front window. The door still stood, and the shutters still held, but the obviously big grizzly had sought entrance into the cabin and failed. His anger showed with the downed poles on the corral, and where he dug in the dirt where the hides had been staked for scraping.

Joseph and Lizzie moved their horses up beside Tatum and the three stared at the damage done. The horses were skittish, apparently smelling the presence of the Grizzly. Without speaking, Tatum slipped from his mount and went to examine the traces of the big beast. As he looked at the carcass, he could tell the kill was several days old, but the bear had returned to his kill and partially buried it, returned and ate more, and then threw more dirt on the carcass to await his return. The tracks showed to be at least a couple days old, well before the snow had come through but here in the clearing, what little snow had fallen had already blown or melted away. The other sign, claw marks and digging also showed to to have been made on the same visit.

Tatum looked at the entry to the cavern and the heavy door he had fashioned, and it appeared to be undamaged beyond a few futile claw marks. He breathed a sigh of relief, knowing the winter's supply of meat was safe. He went to the corral, lifted up a downed pole and replaced it in the double post corner. He looked back at Joseph and Lizzie and said, "See, there's always somethin' to be doin' to make a home a home!"

"Yassuh, and like you said, Freedom is somethin' ya' allus' has to fight for," added Joseph.

The mountains had become his home. He made them his home after fleeing the hypocrisy of civilization in Missouri at the graveside of his father and mother and began fulfilling the life long dream held dear by his father and himself. When he first came to the mountains, he was a younker and a greenhorn, but now he was a seasoned man of the mountains. Returning from a quick trip back to St. Louis, he was again determined to never leave his beloved mountains, the far blue mountains, the Rocky Mountains, the high and lonesome, the only place he could see forever and breathe the air that held not a scent of anything from civilization.

On the trip up the Missouri to Fort Union aboard the steamboat, he befriended an old-timer and well-seasoned mountain man, Knuckles, and the old man agreed to show the newcomer around Crow and Blackfeet country. Tate Saint knew it was always best to learn from someone that knew the different people of the mountains, and this man seemed to know his way around the different tribes never before encountered by Tate in the mountains to the South. But he wanted to explore all the mountains from the Canadian Rockies to the southern Sangre de Cristo. This time the mountains in the north were beckoning the young man so full of wanderlust, but little did he know what awaited, from renegades to missionaries and a lovely Indian lass that seemed to be the answer to the question he didn't know how to ask.

COMING JUNE 2018

GET YOUR FREE STARTER LIBRARY

Join the Wolfpack Publishing mailing list for information on new releases, updates, discount offers and your FREE Wolfpack Publishing Starter Library, complete with 5 great western novels: http://wolf-packpublishing.com/receive-free-wolfpack-publishing-starter-library/

ABOUT THE AUTHOR

Born and raised in Colorado into a family of ranchers and cowboys, B.N. Rundell is the youngest of seven sons. Juggling bull riding, skiing, and high school, graduation was a launching pad for a hitch in the Army Paratroopers. After the army, he finished his college education in Springfield, MO, and together with his wife and growing family, entered the ministry as a Baptist preacher.

Together, B.N. and Dawn raised four girls that are now married and have made them proud grandparents. With many years as a successful pastor and educator, he retired from the ministry and followed in the footsteps of his entrepreneurial father and started a successful insurance agency, which is now in the hands of his trusted nephew. He has also been a successful audiobook narrator and has recorded many books for several award-winning authors. Now finally realizing his life-long dream, B.N. has turned his efforts to writing a variety of books, from children's picture books and young adult adventure books, to the historical fiction and western genres

https://wolfpackpublishing.com/b-n-rundell/

Printed in Great Britain
by Amazon